Beverly Po

# Lineage

Author

**Beverly Post-Schmeler**

Beverly Post-Schmeler - LINEAGE

2012 by Beverly Post-Schmeler.

All rights reserved. No part of this book may be reproduced, stored in a retrieval system or transmitted in any form or by any means without the prior written permission of the publishers, except by a reviewer who may quote brief passages in a review to be printed in a newspaper, magazine or journal.

Printed in the United States of America

ISBN: 978-1-105-44829-4

Beverly Post-Schmeler - LINEAGE

For my husband Tim,
Children and Grandchildren

# Preface

I had a great time writing this book. Although a tale of pure fiction, one has to wonder, where did we all originate? What happened to the feminine part of God?

There is a little bit of the divine in all of us. This is what we use to help us make decisions in this life. To become better people! To make a good contribution to society as a whole! To leave a lasting legacy for those who come after us.

There are many stories concerning the Holy Grail. This one is entirely imaginary, except for a few doses of reality, such the Knights Templar and the places I have named in the book (other than the fictional Irish kingdoms, of course!).

I hope you come away after reading this book at least pondering the questions we've all held inside. What is the truth? Whose truth is the real truth? Will we ever know? I certainly know we will. One day.

## Chapter 1: Fourth Century Ireland

A small group of soldiers sat still on sleek, magnificent mounts in a dense thicket, hidden from sight by a cluster of tall Douglas fir trees.

Quietly they observed a picture play out before them. A stream of women went by, all dressed in long white gowns with bodices edged in gilded gold, as tiaras set with precious stones glittered on their heads. Their long hair, some braided, some hung loose, glinted in the early morning sun. He hoped his men and his horses would not betray them as they strolled near him single file, moving slightly away, but not too far off in the distance. The men saw the old, thick book the first woman carried above her head and wondered if the women knew they were here. If they knew they were being watched. If they knew they were in danger. It wasn't a question of who these women were, stepping out from beneath the last dredges of night. It was what drove them to gravitate toward the dawning of each new solstice as the sun crept up just above the Eastern horizon.

He knew these six women to be the daughters of King Milidh. He was the Celtic ruler of Ireland for the past three hundred years. His family had been kept hidden lest they be slain, for the Romans were everywhere, killing men, women and children who followed the old ways.

"Old, my ass," he thought.

Wasn't there only one way to worship? God and Goddess, Mother and Father, my Lord and Lady. Why is it that this new Rome, this one with only one God, was what they must all follow now? Where was the Mother Goddess? Where is she? Hasn't she been here since time began? But for his life's sake, he kept his Celtic beliefs to himself. It was money that kept food in his belly and these days it was the Romans who had all the money. It was luck, fate, whatever you want to call it, that spoke to him in a dream not two weeks ago, telling him this was the spot where he would find what he sought.

"Go to where the night becomes day. Where sky meets the sea and you shall see."

Eurenni ap O'Mall, at two score and six, was the oldest and wisest of the men who were with him. Seasoned through many battles, he always looked as he did now, dressed in chain mail, a two-edged sword strapped to his side, ballock knife tucked at his waist, and a spare smaller sword dangled from a sheath that hung down his back.

He was a warrior. Standing more than six feet tall, he had dark brown eyes rimmed with long lashes. His chiseled face was seasoned by the sun and wind. A few grey hairs were sprinkled amongst the long brown locks. A sharp, fine nose defined his face, and rippled muscles completed the warrior's makeup. He was quick and clever. His mind and tactics in battle had won him the favour of the Roman Empire. It was this faith that set him apart from the other migrant Celtic soldiers who sought their fame and fortunes away from Ireland and Scotland.

When he was summoned from a battlefield by Rome, he went without question.

When he rode into Rome three months later, he and his beloved mount, Annaini, were exhausted. The road there had been long and dangerous. Many would-be challengers had fallen dead at his feet. The battles were swift and furious. His task to reach Rome was stronger than his attackers' wishes to end his life for a few pence or a stale piece of bread. One's life wasn't worth much in these days!

Upon arriving at the gates of the Roman castle, he was quickly given an audience with his paid ruler. Barely did he have the chance to kneel before him when the Roman Emperor gave him a task so great, so impossible, and so against his soul that he still couldn't believe he had agreed to it. Actually agreed, he mused, is not the word he would use. It was more like, Do it, or I'll use you as bait at our next spectator sport!

And here he sat, hiding in a thicket, ready to murder women for a mythical book. A chill ran down his back, telling him he was not alone here today, waiting to sway the hand of fate.

Thinking back to his meeting with the emperor, he was happy to say he had no aspirations of becoming a gladiator. These poor men had to fight for their lives every moment in captivity. At least he fought for his life every day in the open air, free from chains, free from lions and jeering crowds.

He brought himself back to the present, blinking a couple of times to clear the mist that had invaded and once again set his eyes on the female leader in white.

His gaze drifted up to her delicate hands as they held above her head the book of ages aloft; down over her sun-bronzed arms, taking in the gold torques that glistened on her forearms and neck; down her straight back, where the most beautiful auburn hair he had even seen was hanging.

He thought if he were to run his hands through it, it would be like strung silk. He finished off his inspection by invisibly running his fingers down her long legs to cup her sandaled feet. She was stunning. What was he thinking? He looked around quickly at the other men to see if they had sensed anything from him. From the look on their blank faces, it was true enough they had not. Blowing out a soft breath he turned back to watch the woman and tried not to focus on the lead one, lest his men actually snap to life and slay him here and now!

The women began to sing softly as they passed, chanting a song he well knew in ancient Gaelic. Not for the first time this morning, his heart leapt in remembrance. Sucking in a harsh breath, his men swiftly turned their stoic faces toward him in question. But this time he did not notice. He had flown backward in time to when he was a young boy sitting on his mother's knee in a poor crofters shack. Every night after a meagre meal, she would sing to him of the ancient ways, and love him. Every day then was so simple, spending his days taking care of a few sheep and one cow, gathering fruit from nearby laden forests, and playing with his friends. Life now was so harsh and uncompromising. This land was ruled by the Roman Empire now, not the Pagan empire it once was, he reminded himself. Giving his body a mental shake, he managed a sheepish grin and, nodding at his men that he was back, once more paid intense attention to the goings on around him.

That was stupid, he thought to himself. He had almost spoken out loud the words he promised his mother he would never repeat. His life would be over if he did, in the same way hers was ended so violently many years ago. He missed her still, but to acknowledge it would be suicide. So instead he stalked innocents and, now today, would get the prize the Roman emperor demanded.

The power it held within its pages was unimaginable. It is said that the one who possesses the book lives forever. Fables, he scoffed, dusting off his pant leg to cover up the sudden jerking of his body as it filled with remembrance. It was time to end this reminiscing!

Nodding to his men, he said, "It is time."

The thundering sound of horse's hooves pounding upon the hard earth brought the women up short, and they looked back in fright at the four riders approaching. The leader, Gwitherian, laid a hand on her sister Annatha's arm.

"Do not be frightened, sister," she said softly. "The one who rides in front is not going to harm us. He is going to save us."

"Save us? Sister, do you not see the sword in his hand?" Annatha cried as she tried to drag her sisters into the trees not far off the field.

She was frantic as tears streamed down her face. She was too young to die, wasn't she? Wasn't this the fate her father had feared all these hundreds of years? They were the last survivors. The daughters were the last existing descendants of King Milidh ap McPhilmea's lineage and until this moment, he had been able to keep them safe from harm.

They were kept hidden. It was only on the solstices that they ventured above. They were sheltered beneath the bowels of the earth in an underworld kingdom known only to a precious few, save they, too, be found and slaughtered like lambs as the others had been. Gereth, Adain, Lanneach and Gealib, her four brothers, had been killed along with many uncles and aunts, and her dear Mamann Elisebeth. What became of her mamann's family she did not know!

The last axiom she had been given was that they were spread out amongst the hills and glens of Scotland and Ireland.

She had not heard a word from any of them in so long; she was sure they had all perished. Such was the lust of the Romans to rid the land of any Pagan influences, that to even be a distant relative to a former empire was to know your days were few upon this earth.

Eurenni saw the women stop, saw their look of surprise and fear, even from a distance. He could smell it, taste it, and he knew the foul stench it would make. Invading his nostrils so that never again would he breathe truly clean air again, the disgusting odour would haunt him the rest of his days. The only one who stood her ground was the lead one, the one that captured him from the moment he set eyes upon her.

His men unsheathed their swords as they neared. The metallic scrapping sound jarred Eurenni's nerves so much so that he wanted to slay them himself. What was he thinking? Had he lost his mind? Slay his men?

But that was exactly what he was thinking as he neared the women. Instead of following through with the plan to slay them for the book that he had been paid for, he reined in his horse a few yards away and turned on his men. Such was the flurry and fierceness of his sword that the men in their surprise didn't stand a chance. Within moments they all lay on the ground. Their bodies were broken and blood-soaked.

Gwitherian had watched as the warriors bore down upon them. In that one instantaneous moment she locked eyes with the lead man. She felt a rush of air and heat hit her body. So strong was it that her arms, still holding aloft the book above her head, would not support themselves. They had become like molten lava. Her body trembled, and she could tell by the surprised look on his face that he felt the connection too. She saw him change before her eyes from stranger to one she felt inside she had known a lifetime or more. She witnessed him turn swiftly away from her and her sisters, and with a loud battle cry known only to a few, slew his own men.

She set the heavy book at her feet. The ritual, a moment ago so ingrained in their beings, was now long forgotten. She threw out her arms and ran to her sister's sides. They all cried and hugged each other, not quite believing what just happened. A stranger had spared their lives, one who they were sure, a few moments ago, meant to kill them.

Eurenni looked down upon the slain men and dropped his blood-stained sword on the ground. What had he done? he asked himself. He drew his hands up into his hair and, hugging his head, dropped to his knees and wept. He wept not for the men, as they were just like him, mercenaries. No! He wept for his soul. At that last possible moment when his thoughts of right and wrong were thrown out, he saw in the woman's eyes someone he knew, or did know, and such emotions overcame him. To protect her overtook all other orders or reasonings. Now he wept because he had once again found her.

Gwitherian left her sisters and ran to kneel beside the man. Lightly touching his shoulder, she felt a spark that almost made her pull back. It was compassion that made her hold firm to his body.

"Sir?" she asked quietly. He did not respond but continued to weep into his hands, his body shaking with uncontrolled sobs. "Sir?" She shook him this time until he dropped his hands and looked into her face. Tears were still running down his cheeks.

"Um, I am Gwith—" She stopped speaking when she saw him trying to mouth words. He must be in shock, she thought.

But finally, after a few attempts, he said, "I am Erenni ap O'Mall. I…I…was g-going to. Goddess, I can't believe. I was going to k-kill you. I am s-so s-sorry."

"Stupid question, I guess, but why exactly were you going to do such a thing, sir?"

She was immediately overcome with emotion. She was angry, sad, and grateful and even felt the stirrings, Goddess forbid, of love for this soldier. Pushing herself away from him, she rested backward on her heels and took a large calloused hand in her own. He looked down as the woman's small fingers as they entwined his large ones and reared back again as the past smashed into his present once more.

"Gondall? Gondall, lad, where are you? Your cousins are coming soon!"

Reannine, the beautiful daughter of King Elslid of the Isle of Skye, searched the rooms of their huge castle for her beloved son. She knew he would want to be here when his cousin Annabella came to visit. At eighteen he was about to ask her for her hand, and his mother fully approved of the marriage. As third cousins they were far enough removed as far as she was concerned to have a safe joining and produce heirs. Why, in some kingdoms they were marrying off first cousins! That, she thought, was a bit much ,but to each his own. The Isis garden had been overhauled in preparation for Annabella's acceptance of his proposal, and the wedding ritual she had planned would be exquisite. People would come from all over the Celtic world to witness the joining of the two families. Such was written. Such is the way it would be.

The harsh sounds of steel on steel as horses and riders made their way over the drawbridge and into the inter sanctum of the castle grounds brought her up short to look to the nearest turreted window. She looked down three stories to the cobbled walkway below and saw the carriages pull up to deposit her beloved sister and her brood. She looked on in silence as the first carriage door was opened and a lovely woman with long golden auburn hair stepped out with the help of a footman.

Sensing she was being watched, she turned her emerald green eyes upward and gave a beautiful smile to her future motherin-law. Oh, yes, she knew. She had been told of this joining by the Goddess long ago. Soon the families would be joined and the "Book of Ages" lineage would start once more on its rightful path.

Eurenni's head snapped up as his body returned him to the present to stare into the angelic face of another Goddess. He knew he had just witnessed the past. How? He was not sure, but so many strange things had happened today. What was one more? But he was sure he saw one of his ancestors, who, from what the vision told him, was about to take a bride. Without the need to ask, he knew this woman sitting so calmly in front of him to be the ancestor of Annabelle from his vision and he, with astonishment, knew he was the ancestor of this Gondall.

He looked down again at their entwined fingers and lifted them gently to his lips, pressing a kiss so light and tender that at once tears sprang to Gwitherian's eyes. Molten eyes of emerald green met the deep rich brown of another, and as had been in the past, the rightful families had, despite battles and massacres, survived to meet once again. Love would once more fill the world.

Eurenni and Gwitherian were married a few months after their auspicious encounter and together sired twelve children. The Book of Ages stayed with them, kept safe below the cursed world of the Romans until one day, as fate would have it, their kingdom was stumbled upon by a Roman soldier. He quickly sent word to Rome of his find. A huge army was formed and they besieged the kingdom for months until the last man, woman and child had been slain. The book was never found. But they all had not all died for naught, for one male and one female had been spirited away by a pagan priest so that the lineage would continue two millennia from now.

# Chapter Two France 1307 AD

Gete Zhmaagan had been roaming the lands of Mongolia, upper Tibet and China for many years. Searching for what, he did not know. Yet the journey was one he knew in his soul he must partake of. At five score and five, he was ancient in some circles. In others, nearly mid-way through his life term. He had been on this life journey for 10 years now. He had walked through more countries than he could count.

The world was a strange place, he thought. So many traditions! So many trying to prove their way was the right way. They would consider it their lives vocation to change anyone who would listen, to see their beliefs as blasphemy and convert. It was a dangerous obsession with some men, a passion for others. He kept silent, though. He learned quickly that to reveal ones religion was to welcome death, or worse, torture! The Catholics ruled the lands now. Most of Europe had been converted after the great fire of Rome. Paganism was dead as far as the heralded Pope was concerned. One could only read what the Pope called truth. Even his beloved Ireland, land of the Celts, no longer practiced the old religion. And Scotland, land of the Picts, had fallen to the new Christian ways. The few who escaped the reformation remained in hiding lest they be found out and burnt at the stake.

Such a nasty way to die! he thought.

He had witnessed a young woman die once, wrongly accused, of course. She was simply a *wise woman* who used herbs to heal. They branded her a witch and burnt her alive in the village square.

He stopped walking to remember her, setting his long wooden staff to rest against his shoulder as he looked over the waters of Lac du Pelerin in Poitou-Charentes. The still waters abounded with marine life. Fish leapt at regular intervals as hungry gulls swooped overhead. He wondered aloud, "In a land so beautiful, how can such ugliness exist?"

As if it were yesterday, he saw her in his mind's eye. She had beautiful raven hair, which hung past her waist; velvety soft, creamy white skin; and the bluest eyes he'd ever seen. It was the eyes that brought her to mind now as they matched the waters that lapped on the beach before him.

It happened five years ago as he walked into a small village in England. There was a hustle and bustle in the streets that meant more than it was simply market day. When he managed to stop a person to ask what was happening, he was told happily that a witch was to burn that very afternoon and he should come and watch.

"How long has this been going on?" he asked the stranger.

"What? You mean the burnings?" the stranger replied.

"Yes! Good God! When did we turn so barbaric?" He steamed.

"Who are you, stranger? Why do you ask about what is to all a normal occurance?" the other asked suspiciously.

"I am no one," Gete answered as he shouldered himself away and ran quickly into the crowd. The gathering now pushed and shoved its way into the centre of the village square. Before he realized it he was helpless to leave as a few hundred others had gathered all around him. He knew that, like it or not, he was going to witness the death of a Pagan sister.

He watched them parade her by in an old wooden cart with wooden rungs that acted as her cage. She sat still, her back straight, her head up. She seemed not to hear the jeers or feel the rotten fruit as it pelted against her thin body. The rickety cart came to a stop not ten feet from him, and they dragged her out of it and up a few steps to a wooden platform resting off the ground. They quickly tied her to a wooden stake already placed that had been greased previously with black tar.

"Makes for a better burn," someone in the crowd chortled.

A man in his late forties, with fat jowls and a body to match, stomped up the stairs. He was trying to look important, and carrying a decree that he read aloud to the now hushed crowd.

"It is by order of the Crown and the Pope that this woman, Aneathia McPhellimea, be burned at the stake until she is dead for crimes against the Church and State. She has been accused and convicted of being a witch on this date, June 10, thirteen hundred and second year of our Lord."

The man finished reading the decree, and walked over to the woman and ripped her dress away from her back, revealing a star-shaped birthmark just above her left breast.

"The mark of the beast!" he declared with a loud screetch, and the crowd roared.

Gete's eyes never wavered from the young woman. She, seeing someone in the crowd who was different than the others who were screaming obscenities at her, never took her eyes off him, even after they lit the straw and sticks at her feet.

The burning was quick, but to Gete, it was unmercifully slow. She never cried out as the fire burned away her flesh, but he felt her pain deep inside his being. It was something he knew he would never forget. Nor would he ever forget the mark, the mark that connected them all!

Shaking his head to clear the vision of long ago, he picked up his staff that had fallen to the ground, and took one last look around at the lake. Then he continued on his journey.

Nights were especially lonely for Gete. He had no one most of the time to pass the hours with. Once in a while a stranger would happen by his meagre campsite, and they would share some whisky and stale bread and cheese. If he was lucky, he had a piece of fruit as well, but preferably not the kind with a worm inside!

It was on this day, and in this country, that Gete was to meet the ones that would fulfill the first part of the journey he had been chosen to take.

Asking the locals where he should travel to find the best churches to visit in the area, he was given a list that included the Rennes le Chateau not far from where he now stood. A beautiful place, they said. It was run by some priest and also by the Knights Templar. He didn't know who these men were, and really didn't care, but he wanted to see the church as it was built on top of the grounds where a former Pagan Church once stood. He had found so many of these across Europe that he had given up counting them all.

The roads there were arduous, and by the end of one day's walk his feet were sore and blistered. He was thirsty and starving, so he stopped at an old crofter's cottage to ask if he could lodge with them for the evening.

They saw in him, in his eyes, a man of hope, and quickly opened their door and lives to him. After quick introductions, he discovered they were displaced Celts. Something like me, he thought.

They were displaced. Without a home or family! They were the decedents of an ancient kingdom he had never heard of before. Both of their families, the O'Malls and McPhellmias, have long suffered and held fast to their pagan beliefs despite the dangers each day presented to them.

It was with great sadness he narrated to them the horrible story they not that long ago had him weeping inside. They were horribly saddened but not surprised. She was but one of many who had lost their lives since the Romans took over. He listened intently to their tale and heard also about the church he intended to reach in another day's journey. They warned him the current French King Philip IV was not to be trusted, and he should warn the Templars about him when he met them the next day. He promised he would relay their warnings to them, and after a wonderful meal of hot, fresh bread, ale and grilled fish, he laid to rest on a comfy pallet of fresh straw. It was the first good night's rest he'd had in a very long time. Early the next morning he bid them a fond farewell and once more resumed his journey.

The family watched the old man leave until he was but a speck in the distance. The man and woman in the cottage wrapped their arms around each other and hugged. Their children, and their children, and so on, would have a future now. This they were sure of. They had been told the story of the one who would save the families from extinction, never believing for a moment it would be them who would welcome him into their midst! Happily they now believed their lineage would be safe once more, placed in one man's hands until the next millennia. They sent a prayer up to the Mother Goddess to give him the strength he would need to survive until then.

Gete passed by several small villages the next day. He watched as young children ran after dogs, and women carried baskets of vegetables to and from the markets. Near midday he came across a graveyard at the top of a small hill near the chateau. He stopped to admire the Celtic influences on the gravestones.

The tall Celtic crosses were so beautifully ornate. The stone surfaces were covered in delicate carvings that took years. Their symbolism was lost, even on him. Each cross was marked with a circle on the back, reflecting the Sun God.

"One day they will know the truth," he shouted to the wind. "One day they will all know the truth!" His loud, booming voice startled the nesting birds nearby, and he chuckled as he walked down the hill toward the chateau.

Gete was warmly greeted at the door by a monk and motioned inside to rest and have something to eat. He led him down a long narrow hallway into a much larger room with high vaulted ceilings. The room was quite large and housed a number of long wooden tables with equally long wooden benches to sit on. The monk left him there to get comfortable and returned quickly with a hot bowl of stew and fresh bread. Cheese and fruit topped off the meal. He washed it all down with warm mulled wine. *I must be doing something right,* he mused. *For I haven't eaten as well as I have in the past couple days in at least a year!*

It was getting late, so after only meeting three of the Knights he was shown to a small room in the back tower of the chateau to rest for the night. A small fire was lit in the stone fireplace at one end of the small room, and his bed was a straw mattress up off the floor for more airflow and comfort. Although, the window had shutters, the fire did nothing to keep the room warm. He was grateful when they brought him a second quilt to throw over his chilled legs. In the dead of night he was awakened by shouts and screams. He jumped out of bed quickly and opened the heavy wooden door. Just as he was about to peer out, three men came crashing in his room, sending him sprawling to the floor.

"Vous devez partir maintenant !" the first man said as he bent down to haul Gete quickly to his feet. "You must leave," he repeated again in English.

"Why? What is happening? I heard screams and—"

"Nous sommes massacered! They are killing us!" came the French and English replies.

"Why?"

"Nucun temps! No time! Go now!" He pushed Gete toward the tower window and helped him slip over the window ledge to another ledge just slightly below.

"Arrett! Stop! Wait," the man said above him just as Gete was about to jump to another ledge. The knight above him passed him down a huge book tied to a rope
.
"Garder ce sûr. Ceci est le Livre majeur. Le garder avec vous jusqu'à ce que vous savez que le temps a raison de révéler c'est la vérité. This is the Book of Ages. Keep it safe until you know the time is right to reveal the truth."

Gete reached out, grabbed the book, and uncoiled the rope. He sent it back up to the Knight who had disappeared inside the window. He hoped that by sending it back up to the window quickly, the others would be able to escape.
Gete knew it would be dangerous to wait to see if they, too, were able to escape, so he fled with the book tucked safely inside his worn cloak. He never looked back, knowing this was his destiny. The one he had traveled and searched for without knowing. The Goddess had now entrusted him with the lineage of life, the Book of Ages.
A few hours later, just as the sun was dawning on the horizon, he knew he was far enough away from the chateau to be safe. He found a small cave dug out of a hillside and crawled inside to rest. He laid the book softly upon his lap and opened it to the first page. Suddenly a mass of visions overcame him. He saw the future, what it would be like. The wars…oh, the wars and such strange things!
He could not fathom them until the final page floated down upon him and he smiled. Peace! Final peace was the last

vision, and he knew it would be with his help that the world would finally see it, too. But until then he would have to be patient and make his way out of Europe and travel to North America, where the final showdown would take place a few hundred years from now. In the meantime, though, he had lots of time to get to know this book and make his way there. He couldn't wait! Let the adventure begin!

# Chapter 3 Ontario, Canada 2009

Sitting at her old, battered desk in a cubicle at the far end of a busy newsroom, Elizabeth Constance McPhelimy worked diligently. If it wasn't one thing, it was another, in the crazy city that demanded her attention. Today as she sat finishing up her latest story, little did she know that within moments her life would change forever...

The door of the newsroom suddenly flew open. The vibrating metal clanged off the inner walls, rattling the windows. Breaking into the intense craziness of the newsroom, the noise shattered the prattle and hum instantly.

Eliza was into her third cup of coffee. Her thoughts, her words, her writing had to stay focused entirely within the confines of her space and her work. Her body was hunched over her laptop, fingers flying over the keys as she reported on another crime from within the bowels of her city. Now she would be lucky to finish the story in time, if at all, for the first copy run was in 45 minutes! The unknown asshole who smashed the door open had caused her to jerk her hand sideways as she reached for her coffee cup. She missed grasping the cup fully, and it had spilled its black contents all over her handwritten notes. Looking down at the dripping mess now, she saw the ink-filled words running into each other.

As she seethed she also wanted to cry. Instead, she slammed her fist on the metal desk and jumped up to meet, greet and kill the bastard who she knew had now caused her all kinds of unwanted grief. And perhaps her job! Raising her head above the grey cubicle wall, she yelled, "Hey, dumb ass! Do you realize what you have just done?"

Eliza came around her desk in one quick, fluid motion and raced at the intruder, arm raised and hand fisted, ready to take the world on. The one responsible for her ire had stopped instantly, frozen in place with his mouth agape. In slow motion he paused to stand just inside the doorway, looking around at the startled journalists. He took in the scene of stock-still figures looking like department store dummies. Faces were frozen, eyes glazed and mouths agape. What remained of spilt coffee dripped off several desks onto the tiled floor with a steady plop, plop sound, as another person was trying to put out a small fire caused when he upended an aromatherapy candle into his waste paper-basket.

"Why, I ought to rip your bloody tongue into three pieces while someone crushes your balls with pliers! And then while you are screaming on your knees like a girly man…"

Holding up his hands in self-defense, Jerry pleaded, "Eliza! Whoa! Stop! Wait a sec, will ya? Let me explain!"
He backed himself up against the wall, ready to fight her off if need be. Deep inside that is what he was secretly hoping for.

But at the same time, he was scared shitless at the sight of a woman with PMS breathing imaginary fire and brimstone as she came at him like governor/actor Slazenger from the movies. But this was important shit! She would change her tune shortly! This he was sure of!

"Eliza, wait! Don't…UGH!"

His next words were quickly cut off as the wind was ripped from him from a hard sucker punch to his gut.

"W-why did you do that?" he gasped as he sunk slowly to his knees onto the cool tiled floor.

He heard snickers from all corners of the room as he raised his head and squinted up at his co-worker standing over him, ready to give him another rude awakening.

"Why? Why did I give you a dose of reality? You have to ask?" she screeched as she shook her fist in his face.

"You have just ruined my notes, you maniacal result of Clockwork Orange! Oh, but not just any notes, but the ones I was half done typing, and now they are ruined! Jake is going to have my ass when I can't turn in the story on the Kingsway killing in 30 minutes. And it's your fault. That's why!"

Eliza was breathing so heavily that she took a step away and leaned back against a desk next to the door, extending her arm briefly against the doorframe for support.

She then bent over, grasping her knees as she tried to gain control. Jerry Richard Malloy was the young reporter from Montreal who had started working for The Toronto City Tribune only a few weeks ago. He was new, yes, but there were rules to follow here! He needed to learn and learn quickly what was and was not acceptable behaviour in the newsroom. She was about to take it upon herself to educate him!

"Dorothy's dead," came the quiet reply from the floor.

Her head whipped up so quickly she was surprised it didn't snap right off!. For effect, and her own confirmation, she felt around her neck to be sure all was still attached.

"Dorothy's dead? Dorothy? O-our Dorothy?"

When Jerry sat mutely and simply nodded his head, all fight left her. Like a deflated balloon, she sank to the floor beside him.
Grabbing the sleeve of his white shirt, more for support than affect, she asked in a voice that for a moment failed her, "How? What happened?"

Her throat felt parched, and her voice sounded small and far away to her eyes. The buzzing in her ears became so loud she was sure the whole world could hear it. Black dots began to swim in front of her eyes. Jerry's voice came through as though he were at the far end of a tunnel.

"How? Why? God, what the hell happened, Jerry?"

"The cops said it was a suicide. A situation they called it, similar to how her Mom died back in the '60s. Nice explanation, huh? That's all they gave me. No more, no less! Then they not quite politely asked me to get the hell out of there. I heeded the call and came straight here to see you."

The weight of it all was just starting to sink into his young mind, and his hands shook as he ran them through his hair.

"Listen, I'm sorry about the door," he spoke quietly. "I was in a hurry and didn't think. Actually, I was more in shock. I can't believe it! I went there to pick her up, since her car quit working last night. She called me just last night! GOD, Eliza! It just doesn't make sense. She was fine. Pissed, but fine. Not suicidal! When she didn't answer her doorbell I tried the knob. It was open, so I went inside, calling her name."

He recoiled internally as his mind tried to come to grips with the scene he saw playing out before him again. He didn't even realize he was speaking verbally what his mind saw.
"I went from room to room, calling her name. I saw her purse on the telephone table, so I knew she was there or was there not long ago. It was so quiet, but I didn't expect to see…didn't think I'd see…her…she was sitting up in her bed, Eliza! A book was perched on her lap like she was getting ready to settle in for the night. Does that make sense to you? Well, does it?" he asked her questioningly, his blue eyes tearing up.
As he was speaking his usually quiet voice had begun to rise as the incredibility of it all began to sink in. He looked up and around at the blanched faces of his colleagues and then came back to Eliza.
He continued to watch her mutely as she pushed herself up

to a standing position, rocking on shaking legs, and looked around the room. Some of her female co-workers were already openly crying; work forgotten, as others simply stood there with stunned looks on their faces. They were like any other band of co-workers who functioned in the public sector. They were close-knit, bonded to each other in ways many wouldn't understand. To lose one was to lose a piece of you. They were family. She reached down and extended her hand to him, which he readily accepted. He stood up beside her. Her anger, which moments ago had been a huge affair, had dissipated as quickly as it began. Now was a time to bond together, she thought. They would need each other's strength more than ever in the coming moments, days and weeks ahead. Instinct told her what was happening now was only the beginning. The beginning of Goddess knows what, and fighting now just seemed so petty in the face of such sadness.

The tears came without warning, spilling down her cheeks and dropping on her blue blouse. Tiny droplets speckled the silky fabric like a sudden rainstorm. Jerry stood there, looking at her, not knowing quite what to do. Should I hug her or hold her? He thought to himself.

He marveled for a moment that it didn't matter how or where you came from, a newsroom came together quickly in the face of tragedy. He gave himself a shake and then slid a comforting arm around her, allowing her to lay her sobbing body against his. They were huddled this way when Jake sauntered into the room.

"All right, you slugs. No time for sex. We have a paper to get to print! Malloy, get your hands off the pretty reporter and get me that story on the gas explosion at Union E." He spoke to Eliza without turning to face her. "It's not the time or place! Get it together. I need your story on my desk and ready for print in ten minutes! And the rest of you, get back to work!" Without looking back, he stalked into his office at the end of the edifice.

The slamming of his office door seemed to kick the people back into action. The beginning sounds of rustling paper and doors being opened and closed began and then the familiar drone of keyboards and phones filled the air as everyone except Eliza and Jerry shook off the horror of a few moments ago and went back to reality.

Eliza slowly extracted herself from Jerry's arms and, dragging her arm across her face in a jerky motion to clear the tears, stalked off in the direction of the boss's office. The anger that had faded a moment ago when she heard the news exploded back to the surface with intensity. She strode in without knocking, and he looked up in surprise at the intrusion.

"What the hell?" he blustered, looking around her to see if any more people followed. He reacted just in time to see the "axis of evil" heading toward him. For once, words failed him.

Without waiting for her boss to open his mouth, Eliza charged in to dish out her tirade. She pushed aside a plump office chair, which sat just inside the office at a right angle to the desk, and stood nose to nose with him, daring him to speak. She was daring him to breathe before she had a chance to let it all out with both barrels blazing. When the shocked look didn't leave his face, she knew this moment was hers and jumped right in.

"WHAT KIND OF PERSON ARE YOU?" she shouted,

slamming both hands on the desk in front of her, making him jump backward in his chair.

"Dorothy's dead! You remember her? She's one of your employees! She's dead and all you can do is come in the place and treat us all like a piece of meat? Is this all you care about? This damned paper? Well, how's this for anews flash, buddy! I QUIT! Get some other lackey who has no heart to do your damn stories. I'm finished!"

Eliza turned away without another word and left his office by way of another slamming door, just to cement the deal. Still shaking inside, she went back to her old desk, grabbed her soft leather jacket, handbag and briefcase and left the startled newsroom without a backward glance.

She exited the building in a daze, swaying from the aftershock, and leaned against the cold stone of the building. She let the coolness of the wall permeate her being. She felt nauseous. Was her world beginning to spin out of control? How did she get down here?
Did I take the stairs or the elevator? She was confused. She raised her head and took in the hustle and bustle of Bay Street, and squinted against the bright sun bouncing off the pristine white sidewalk.

"The world has gone mad," she said aloud as she shook her head in disbelief.

Words began to roll about inside her head. Rolling and swirling around her, feeding off the energy and adrenaline that ran through her veins. "It goes on like nothing has happened while mine is unraveling. Dorothy's dead and no one cares.

Least of all that pariah of a boss I had. I probably wasn't totally fair to him, as he might not have known Dorothy was dead yet until I let him have it! But if he did, then calling him a pariah wasn't good enough!"

The realization that she had just quit a very lucrative job didn't faze her .She was a great reporter! She would find another quickly enough. The Chicago Times had been courting her for months. She might just give them a call. But first she had to find out what happened to her friend. She had enough money tucked away not to have to worry about her bed and breakfast for a while. She pushed her body away from the building and stepped to the curb. Raising her arm, she hailed a cab.

# Chapter 4

"Eliza wait! Hold up, will ya?"

She turned around toward the voice just as she was about to get in the cab. She saw Jerry leaving the building and running toward her.

Dejectedly, she hung her head. Great, she thought. Just what I need! The last thing she wanted to do right now was talk to anyone.

Suddenly exhausted, all she wanted to do was escape. She didn't want to think, speak or deal with anyone, especially Mr. Upstart. This was too crazy, too nuts. Nothing like what had just happened was in her life plan! It wasn't in Dorothy's life plan either!

"OH GOD, Dorothy!" Her heart screamed in pain. "Why? Why did you have to die?" she sobbed.

Dorothy was her friend! She had been 30 years her senior, but they had been close.

Instead of getting in the cab, she set her briefcase down on the sidewalk and waited for him to reach her, knowing that no matter how she was feeling at the moment, she had to give him this time. After all, he was the one who found her friend, and he must be feeling as shitty as she was right now.

He could tell by her stance she wasn't happy to see him, and it hurt him more than he cared to admit. He hadn't known her long, but whether he wanted to or not, he had fallen quickly in love with her. It could be only that new job attraction, but inside he knew it wasn't. They had clicked, or at least he had clicked with her from that very first day not three weeks ago. She was beautiful. Large emerald green eyes lay in a face framed by bright auburn hair, which flowed past her shoulders. Delicate hands belied the warrior within, and she had legs that went on forever. On top of that, she had a smile that took his breath away. Who wouldn't fall in love with her? Many of the single guys at work already had, and a few married ones, too. But she never let on she noticed and perhaps that was another reason.

He reached her in a few quick strides after he saw she was going to wait for him. His heart lurched at the sight of her. Her one hand was still on the cab's open door handle, the other hanging loosely at her side. Her pale face was tear-stained and her eyes rimmed in red. If he wasn't a man, he was sure he would look teary-eyed, too. Actually, if anyone had seen him a couple hours ago, the term "girly-man" would have been appropriate!

"Can I hitch a ride with you?" he asked. "We need to talk about this, Eliza!"

"Listen, Jer," she interrupted, raising her hand off the car door to stop him from speaking.

"I am really not in the mood for company. I just want to go home and bury my head and…"

"Yeah, I know," he interrupted her, doing his best to keep his voice calm and quiet. "I know you want to be alone, but now is not the time. Something is wrong here and we're reporters! We don't usually take a back seat and believe all we're told, do we? Where is your instinct?"

She rounded on him as fast as a bull cornered by a bunch of circus clowns.

"My instinct? You really want to know where my instinct is?"

She was screaming at him now and didn't give a damn that people stopped and stared. To hell with the bombastic Torontonians! What do they know? All they care about are fancy cars and fancy lives, saying the politically correct thing, and doing the politically correct thing no matter how much of their own morality is compromised.

"My instinct is in the morgue with my best friend! Oh, God, I can't believe she's dead, Jerry." She looked up at him, her voice softening as tears began to run once more down her face.

"Why?" she cried. "Why is she dead, Jerry?" Without thinking, she flung herself into his arms.

"That's what I want us to find out," he said as he wrapped his arms around her, lifting a soft curl that had fallen across her forehead.

"You in?"

He could see the wheels turning in her head. The professional Eliza was snapping back. She looked up at him with her green eyes and simply nodded her head. Unraveling herself from his arms, she sank onto the back seat of the cab. She resigned to the fact that whether she wanted him to be with her or not, he was now. Deep inside she was happy she wasn't facing this tragedy alone. He grabbed her briefcase from the sidewalk and ran around the other side of the cab and slid in beside her.

As the car quickly sped away from the curb, a man moved out from the shadows next to the news building and spoke quietly into his cell phone. His eyes never left the cab as it pulled away. Speaking the car's tag numbers into his unit, he dragged slowly on his cigarette and blew the billowing smoke up into the air. It has begun again, he mused to himself. The chase was on, and oh, how he loved the chase!

# Chapter 5

As he lounged back against the bricked wall of the office building, the man some called "The Chameleon" due to his ability to blend into the scenery, flipped open his silver compact phone and dialed another number. He waited for the other end to pick up while he dragged slowly on another cigarette. Simultaneously he took in his surroundings with his flinty, weathered eyes. As soon as the call had begun it was over and, snapping his cell phone shut quickly, he stepped onto the sidewalk and melted into the crowds on Yonge Street. He looked no different than the millions who transverse the same pavement each day. Dressed in a long dark blue windbreaker, shiny shoes and telltale shades to stave off the glare of the Canadian sun, his close-cropped hair was the only giveaway that he wasn't simply your run-of-the-mill businessman. He walked too straight, his shoulders back, head high and hands clenched at the ready. Shaded eyes smoothly glancing from side to side, his head stayed mobile. He was seasoned. An expert. Mabus loved the intrigue and the danger the "job" threw at him. It was the perfect job for the ultimate Type-A personality, whereby every moment of each day, with each breath he drew, he knew it might be his last. This suited him just fine. Dying didn't scare him. Killing was nothing more to him than eating. It was the life he chose.

One day you pick up the spoon or the gun as it were, and just do it. Others wondered how it was that people like Mabus came to be. How can people like this kill without thought, morality or empathy? To know this is to know Mabus and those like him. Born in East Berlin in 1943, at the height of the Second World War, guns and death were the norm. He witnessed it every waking moment. He grew up with and became accustomed to it. The allies had killed his family in a raid one fateful January evening, and the young Mabus was orphaned. He spent the next year of his life on the cold, mortar-gouged streets. He was like thousands of other children without a home, food or love. It made him hard. Made him cold. He died inside the day his family was murdered by the allies. This deeply ingrained hatred made him the cold-hearted killer he was today.

It was only a matter of time before Mabus sickened of his life in Berlin, and headed away from the death and despair, catching the first train he came across.

He traveled the long, lonely rails for weeks at a time, living only on what scarce food and water others would share or he could steal.

By age twenty-five he had found a new life and identity in the Middle East. It was on this journey in mid-1960 that he met up with The Cooperative. The group of very rich Eastern men wanted to ensure the world shared their version of creation and lived by their code of morality and values. In their world all women were submissive and had no role in their church or society. Their ideals were their life's breath, and they slowly molded this lost, emotionless boy into an even colder man. After a great many years, Mabus had another family.

Mabus started off working for them, delivering insignificant items for the organization to their many business partners, until he was able to gain their trust. A few years passed and he was given hit and run deliveries into former Mongolia. His job was to place packages in open spaces where many people would be gathered. He never asked what it was he delivered. He never wanted to know.

He wasn't a stupid assassin. It was his wits that had kept him alive this far, so when he was contracted to take on more duties within the organization, he jumped at the chance. His first job was shadowing Canadian Prime Minister JPK and his illustrious bevy of beauties. A couple of kills later, the Canadian intelligence community was a mess. But, thanks to him, they had a dead PM. He even found them a lackey to blame. What could be more perfect? Convincing other stooges to take out the stooge had been simple enough. Money dusted upon eager palms was sickening but necessary. Too easy, he thought at the time. But then again, it was money that paved the slippery hands, and everyone wanted it. Murder didn't come cheap!

The real mission was revealed to him not long ago when he had taken over the major kills in the world. Protecting their way of life and their radical views was what kept his bank account at ridiculous levels. What did he care if a few more people died? It was all stupid as far as he was concerned. He didn't really care who was right and who was wrong, as long as they paid him well.

Lineage, my ass! He thought. But he played along. Let the big men with their big money believe what they want. He had given up believing in God a long time ago.

# Chapter 6

Eliza was quiet throughout the cab ride, and Jerry didn't press her for conversation. There was plenty of time for him to give her his ideas about Dorothy's death without giving the Asian cab driver some amusement in his day. He suggested they go to a coffee shop instead of her apartment. An old native ran a shop on the eastern edge of the city. It was the only place you could still smoke indoors. The guy had fought in the courts that it was sacred ground, and he could do whatever he wanted in there. So the precious few who still lit up and were fortunate enough to know about the place gave the old guy lots of business.

The cab pulled into the paved parking lot of the ancient-looking business. The huge, white sign above the door read WELCOME TO WILLY'S. The outer walls were made of rough-hewn logs filled with white mortar. Only four windows graced the building, and they were all along the side that faced the Humber River. The owner had placed tables out there on the deck for those who found the stifling, smoke-filled air inside his shop too much to bear at times. Jerry was one of them. He loved to smoke, but too many smokers in one room tended to gag him. He got out first and went around to pay off the driver as Eliza slowly exited out the back door.

She looked exhausted beyond reason. And looking at her made him suddenly feel that way, too. Too much had happened in such a short time, and instinctively he knew inside that this was only the beginning of something big. Perhaps bigger than anything he had ever encountered in his short 24 years. But until he filled her in, she would have no idea how huge this really was. He was suddenly impatient and took her arm to hurry her inside. He ordered two large black coffees and steered her out the back door to sit at one of the white resin tables already set up for the day's early crowds. He was relieved to see they would be alone. The place was deserted. It was barely ten in the morning. Most people were at their jobs, desks laden with steaming cups of morning coffees, teas and cappuccinos as they hunkered down to another working day in the city.

They sat in a troubled but companionable silence for a few minutes, both sipping their coffees as they stared at the flowing waters of the Humber. Sea gulls screamed and swooped overhead at invisible morning meals as the hums and horn blasts of distant traffic filled the air. Jerry forced himself to sit quietly until he sensed from her that it was time to talk. When she signalled for a refill he shook his head to clear the webs and began.

Setting his mug aside, he quietly said, "Uh, I don't know where to start, but at the beginning is as good a place as any, I expect."

She almost jumped out of her skin when she heard him speak. She was so lost in her own thoughts that she had almost forgotten he was there. Almost! Why were they here? Why was he there with her? So many questions and no simple answers, and the sadness that existed moments ago once more threatened to overwhelm her. She picked up her black leather bag and, grabbing a tissue from inside the front pocket, dabbed at her eyes and loudly blew her nose.

"OK." She sniffed. "Tell me. Tell me everything from the beginning, and then I am going to visit the mortician. I have to see her with my own eyes. I think it will be the only way I'll ever believe she is gone."

He relayed every detail he could remember from that morning, from how he got to Dorothy's apartment around 6:30 a.m. until the time he called 911 and spent the next hour giving his report to the police. He wondered out loud how quickly they had arrived and how fast the report had come down the tube about it being a suicide. When he questioned the on-site detectives about their quick reasoning, he was told he was no longer needed, not to leave town, and keep his mouth shut unless he wanted to go the "The Don" for questioning. That was enough for him. The Toronto Don Jail was not known for its cupcake atmosphere, so he had backed off. He noticed Eliza had gone from slouching in the plastic chair to sitting up straight to learning toward him. He knew that intense gaze meant she smelled something rotten. And it wasn't the Humber River making that particular smell!

Taking another gulp of her coffee and setting the cup down, she kept her hands around it as if to warm her still-chilled body.

"OK. I agree with you," she said. "Something isn't right here! When you came into the newsroom you mentioned that it was just like what happened to her mom in the '60s. What did you mean by that? Dorothy never mentioned anything about her family to me, and I've known her for ten years!"

Eliza put aside her grief temporarily after hearing his side of the story. She needed more coffee and a smoke. She had quit years ago, but now seemed the right time to have a puff. She grabbed his pack and lighter off the table, drawing out a pristine cigarette. How could something that looked so good be so bad for you? She mused. Lighting up, she almost gagged as she inhaled, feeling momentarily lightheaded. She had to ask him to stop and repeat what he just said, as it was lost in translation as far as she was concerned.

After the first few sickening puffs, and a few hacking noises, the cigarette took on a familiar taste. She drew on it as they went over the details again and again, musing how quickly people became hooked on these things. Jerry signaled again for coffee refills and an order of bagels. The courteous waiter who was the son of the owner left quickly to fill their order.

"OK, so tell me about Dorothy's mom. What does she have to do with this?" she asked as she drank her new steaming coffee and lit another cigarette.

"Dorothy's mom was none other than famous reporter Charity Stringer." Seeing her quizzical look, he said, "You know the reporter who was a good friend of the Swedish actress Olga Hanson? She was a special friend of the then-Prime Minister James Finnegan Kane? Charity was also a panelist on What's my Story, a popular game-type political show on the CTC back then."

"Nope. Sorry. Doesn't ring a bell. I mean, I know of this late movie star and, of course, the late PM. It is the only assassination we've ever had in Canada, but this was a bit before my time, you know!"

She smiled now for the first time in what felt like days. She liked this young rogue reporter! He had a finely boned face, and great hair. It reminded her of always being windblown, with locks that were always wind-tossed and curly. It was mostly brown with blond highlights from the sun, not from some cheap box bought from a downtown drugstore. She liked the awesome smile with straight, even teeth and, even more interesting, his tongue ring. She had never kissed anyone with a tongue ring before! She pushed herself forward in her chair, jolted by her thoughts and not liking where they were heading. With a mental shake she asked him to continue.

"All right. Back in the '60s, when the show was popular, Charity was a regular. She was also a great reporter for the Ottawa Times and was with the 'in' crowd in the French Quarter for all big-name functions. She knew a lot of celebrities and politicians and so on. She and movie star Olga Hanson became friends, and she was what some may call her 'confidant.' She was also her lesbian lover!"

"NO WAY!" she said, grabbing his wrist. "Olga was gay?" "Yep!" he said, "Not that anything's wrong with that" he added. Immediately feeling a warm, tingling sensation where her small hand wrapped itself around his arm. Clearing his throat, he tried to sound normal.
"Ahem, well, bisexual, actually. JPK found out and tried to end their affair. When she said she'd tell the world they were having an affair…like no one else knew…he panicked. She knew so much more than anyone else figured she did.

She had a lot of information and secrets, which she confided to Charity. Charity was also married to Dan Stringer, the astronaut. You see a pattern here yet?"

She shook her head, but not convincingly.

"No? Okay, lets draw some dots then, shall we?

"PM has affair with movie star."

"Yes, that I know."

"PM tells her stuff that he shouldn't."

Uh huh…got that..too..." She faked a yawn.

"She tells her female lover and then She, Olga, and the reporter end up dead! Suicide, they say. Olga is found dead, sitting up in bed, book in lap. Charity is found dead, also sitting up in bed with a book on her lap, just like Dorothy. Suicide is the reason given for all three deaths. We know Ms. Hanson was a drug user, but according to the files I read, Charity and Dorothy didn't drink or do drugs, so to say they OD'd is a farce! Charity also had several journals that were never found. Dorothy is her daughter. It has been speculated back and forth that her husband found these journals. Then he hid them away, to be given to Dorothy when she got older. Back to her mom, though, He, the prime minister, panics and gives the word that Olga's lover must die, too, to protect federal secrets. Her husband doesn't know she is bisexual, and he is also a member of the lunar landing team whom, even at that time, heard the rumours that the mission was faked. He was fighting his own war, so to speak."

"Oh my God Are you saying it goes that far back?" she interrupted, sitting forward so fast in her cheap plastic chair that the legs bent inwards.

"I haven't had time to really investigate this. I only got a full hour in at the archives after finding Dorothy dead before I came to the paper. I knew right away I was on to something when I found the connection to her mom and Olga. So I would say it goes back further! I believe it pre-dates any PM we've ever had, back to who held a secret about the lineage of mankind!"

"OK, now you've lost me. How can it go as far back as that? I've heard the stories but…well…what does a long-deceased Canadian PM have to do with this? Are you saying this is about the much-ballyhooed Davidic line, the lineage of King David all the way down the line to Mary and then Jesus? I've read about this in several books but never quite believed it."

"Yes and no!" he said, rubbing his temples.

"Huh?" she said, now totally confused.

"OK. Well, some of this is fact, some is hype, and some of this is just my theory, OK?"

"Uh, OK, big guy," she agreed, nodding her head and taking another bite from her bagel.

"Some say George Washford, our first PM, had some secret papers that showed the true lineage of us all. Nothing was ever proven, but it's been said these secret documents were passed on to a good Catholic family, the Kanes.

They were a Celtic family with heredity that is documented back to the first century. Their history is, of course, tragic, as well all know. Many members had early deaths and were caught up in scandal after scandal. But personally I've always felt our first lineage came from Mary and then through her relationship to Jesus it continued on. He was to be the saviour, or so we are told. But whose truth are we buying into here? If you know anything of Celtic, Greek or Egyptian mythology, then you know the Biblical story is true plagiarism of stories told for centuries in those places."

"OK, now this is really getting weird!" she said, trying to piece it all together, but not succeeding. This was just too fantastic.

"I don't know about your theory on lineage," she said as she brushed her hair back from her face, "but we Canucks do know our own history more than the Americans do, or else I wouldn't even have a clue who you were talking about, presidentially, or Prime Ministerarily speaking, of course. Can you imagine if someone asked any American if our PM, Joe Clarkson, was involved in something like this? They would say, 'Joe who?'"

She laughed as she said this, and brushed the windblown hair out of her deep green eyes. Taking her shades out of her purse, she slipped them on and quietly sat back in her chair to take this all in.

Suddenly a whiff of air lifted the hair off the back of her neck, making her instantly aware of her surroundings. She looked back toward the windows of the coffee shop and asked Jerry how well he knew the owners of this place.

"I know them fairly well," he replied as he leaned back in his chair. "I went to U of T with Bill, our waiter. He is smart as a tack and great with computers. We were actually thinking of going to law school together. But he quit third year into a four-year degree program to come and help his father, who is getting quite old. Why?"

"I just wondered," she said, eyeing him again. "I know he was listening to our conversation and since I am a huge conspiracy theorist in all its glory, I was concerned he may be listening for some info to pass on to the cops."

"Why would he do that?" he questioned. His brows furrowed as he tried to discern her reasons for jumping to that conclusion. "I would trust my life in his hands and his father's. They are honourable native people. And they hate the cops. So no worries there in my opinion. They are anti-establishment. Just about anti-anything actually. They are about as far left as you can get. Trust me, you have no worries here. This is why I brought you here. It is what the CIA would call sterile, a safe place where there are no listening ears that can hear you."

"This must be your tender way of telling me I have nothing to worry about, but I still shy away from those I don't know. And I don't know him, but somehow, for some reason, I trust you!" Eliza said.

"Strange…" she continued" "as I don't usually trust people whom I barely know. So consider this a seal of approval, my friend. I don't trust easily. I am also one of those who don't believe the USA landed on the moon, speaking of that astronaut! I know it was a joint Canada/USA thing, but I never believed they did it. It was and still is a huge cover-up. I am bred from the same stock. My mom was kicked out of a Grade 7 science class for refusing to believe it when they showed it apparently "live" on the classroom television set. So, you see, this non-belief that they landed on the moon transcends age groups, countries and governments. The Russians at that time had the know-how to listen to the joint mission as the crap was fed to the world, and I believe they were held hostage for the information they knew. It is still probably being held over the government's head, as the truth has never come out. Makes you wonder how the Russian economy now thrives even though they don't have the might of the former Soviet Union, eh? Can't all be due to joining the European Collective!"

"Anyway," she continued, "sorry about getting off topic a bit, but my mom gave me enough info on the subject for me to believe she is telling the truth. Actually, she finds it hard to believe I am a reporter! She feels it is we, the media that along with the governments of the world only report what they want reported. We're all part of the cover-up, and I actually believe some of that to be the truth. You hear about planes going down with important people on them, mechanical failures cited as the reasons. You hear about banking problems and wonder where your money has gone, and then it magically appears again. You hear about people gambling their lives away in government-run casinos, oil markets zooming out of control, genocides and famines, and you wonder who controls it all. We have enough medicine to wipe out AIDS worldwide, and leprosy. Yet the pharmaceutical companies, as rich as they are, won't give the needy the drugs they need to cure them. Do you ever wonder who they are?"

"Yeah, I do sometimes." He agreed nodding his head.

"Well? What do you think?"

"Didn't I just tell you?" He laughingly asked. But upon seeing her solemn face, he cleared his throat, wiped the smirk off his face and said, "Uh, yeah of course I thought about it a lot a few hours ago when the cops were interrogating me! I wondered why all the hoopla just because I was asking what I thought was some pretty logical questions!" He turned to watch the lazy bobbing of an old log as it floated by on the water.

"But most of the time I am too busy with the here and now to care about all of that bullshit, and I suppose that is the same for most people. If you are right, then that is just what they want us to do. What do you say we head out? I am pretty much coffeed up and starting to shake around the edges. I need to take a walk or something. But I suppose first things first. You ready to leave?"

He watched her face become animated, as if the emotions were breaking through to swallow her whole again. He wondered at how just as quickly she garnered them under control. A mask was a good thing to have right now, and hers was in place.

Nodding, she got up from the plastic chair that she was sure had left a ring around her butt underneath her skirt, and took her billfold from her purse. She looked up when she felt his hand upon her arm to see him shaking his head. He handed Bill a twenty for their coffee and bagels.

She smiled her thanks, and they walked around the outside of the building to the front instead of going inside to the now-packed coffee shop. She looked at her watch and was shocked to see it was past 12:30! They had been there almost three hours and it felt like just minutes.

"Wait here while I go inside to call us another cab. I forgot my cell phone," Jerry said as he left her standing outside Willy's in the bright sunshine. He stepped over the weathered steps. A small bell rang as he pushed open the wooden door of the shop.

# Chapter 7

A dark blue sedan sat in the shadows under a huge maple tree, just far enough down the street to be out of sight, but close enough to watch Willy's. From their vantage point they could see who entered and who left without the need of binoculars. The two men inside the dark car had instructions to watch only. They were not to intercept or draw attention to themselves in the meantime until further word came down from above. It was always this way in covert operations. Watch. Wait. Listen. Follow. X-ray and Delta were old army buddies from Vietnam. They joined Covert upon their return to the USA, when they were faced with hatred from their fellow countrymen and women. It wasn't their fault they failed overseas! They just followed orders and did their dirty deeds all in the name of Uncle Sam. So why were they made to feel they were maniacal, no longer worthy of being a U.S. citizen? Instead of being loved and respected, they were now despised. Only a few were chosen. Many committed suicide, became addicted or homeless, but some were lucky. X-ray and Delta were two of the lucky ones. Their real names hadn't been used in so long they knew they wouldn't answer to them. Codes were the key to life and death. And they were good at staying alive. The static from their shoulder transmitters hummed as they sat in companionable silence and listened. They were primitive compared to today's electronics but were the only type anyone else listening couldn't pick up. The channels were locked. Cell phones weren't safe.

They waited for the code that told them it was time to take this to the next level. It hadn't come, and the operatives knew their "blind date" would be stood up. This mission was a God mission. The orders came only from the Top. If CSIS, the Canadian Security Information Service, found out they were following around a couple of their citizens without their approval, all hell would break loose. But this was bigger than CSIS! It involved the FBI, CIA, MI5, FSB (Russian Security Force), Scotland Yard, Al Amn Al-Khas (Iraqi security), and Cheng Pao K'O (Chinese security). A lot was at stake, was all they were told. Global security! It was always a global thing. It was enough to warrant the risk of a diplomatic fiasco from the Canadian Police Security force, as far as the American gods were concerned. They would be told if this mission was taken up a notch, but not until then. It all depended on what these two they were instructed to follow found out. If they discovered nothing, then they would disappear, melt back into the scenery, and catch the next flight to Washington from Peterson International Airport, and no one would ever know they were here.

Delta spoke quietly into his radio transmitter, relaying the information that suspect number two, the female, had exited the building. Suspect number one had gone back into building. He gave his GPS info to the unknown voice and waited.

They were hoping the suspects under surveillance would go to a place where they could set up a parallel line. A hole in the wall where a method of telephone, telex, cell communications eavesdropping could be done without detection. Unfortunately, there was no time to set it up inside the coffee shop. The best they could get was a bit of scrambled information heard over the rush of water and gulls. It was not enough to discount these two as a security risk or, worse case scenario, eliminate them.

"X," Delta said as he reached inside his suit jacket to adjust the gun holster that had started to stick him uncomfortably in the side. "What do you make of these two? We've been on enough operations to know who is a threat and who isn't. We had to eliminate that Dorothy Stringer woman. We were told to take her out. She was a threat. But I don't see how these two are connected."

"They don't pay us to analyze," X-ray said as he yawned and stretched his arms over his head.

He felt confined. He hated the suits. Always did. He preferred jeans and a t-shirt to these dark "bad boy" outfits. He detested waiting in cars. His ass was growing stiffer with each passing moment. It didn't matter how luxurious the car was, his cheeks always bothered him. A memento from 'Nam!

There was a lot about this job he hated, but it was the money he loved. They were paid six figures a year to do the "unknown's" bidding. Asking questions simply led to more questions and death. He learned long ago to keep his mouth shut when his former partner asked the wrong person the wrong question and ended up in a meat grinder. He still remembered the newspaper headlines: "Man falls to His Death in Freak Accident!" Yeah, it was a freak accident all right, he mused.

"Listen, D. They pay us to keep our traps shut and do a job most other humans with a conscience wouldn't dream of doing." He turned in the seat to face him and said, "It doesn't pay to use our collective brain cells on something we have no control over, OK?"

"Yeah, sure, buddy." He nodded. "Wait, here comes the guy," he said as he sat forward on the leather seat.

His eyes and hands were at the ready for anything that might come up. Training, they called it. First-rate. It was the only kind you get from years of experience in the field.

They sat and listened as their mini-satellite transformer stuck unobtrusively on the side mirror, picked up the couple's conversation.

"I called a cab, Eliza. It should be here in ten minutes or so. Bill offered to drive us, but I told him we were okay," Jerry said as he shoved his hands deep into his front jean pockets.

"That was nice of him. I forgot my cell was in my purse. We could have used it," she added as she looked up and down the street for the umpteenth time. Not once did she notice the sedan, which blended into the scenery so well it was almost invisible. That was why the two men had chosen that vantage point in the first place.

"No problem. No wonder you forgot about it with all that has happened today. What is it? Do you see something?" he asked, following her lead as he looked up and down the busy street.

He did catch sight of the car, though, and turned away as not to attract their attention. He kept it visible through the corner of his eye. He was sure the glare from her Ray bans had reflected off the metallic paint of the car, making it appear holographic and therefore indiscernible to her eyes. But not his!

"Don't look now," he said as he bent toward her ear and whispered, "But there is a car parked about 500 yards down the street." He bent down and whispered into her ear.

"My guess is they are watching us. And from my brief glance, I would say there are two people inside. Suits, and it has government or at the very least, undercover police written all over it. Believe me now?"

He moved closer to her side and with his arm around her shoulders, steered her back toward the building. "I think we should wait for the cab inside." He said as he easily guided her closer to the front door of Willy's.

"Uh yeah, Mr. Spy Guy! Good idea!" she whispered back and allowed him to lead her to the steps.

"You watch way too much TV, McPhelimy!" he retorted.

"Shit! They made us! This is Delta," One of the suits from the car said, speaking rapidly into his shoulder receiver. "We are terminating the lead. X-ray to go pavement artist."

"No," Came the instant reply. "Tell him to stay put. We have a second car in the ring. They are going to take over now. Leave the area immediately." The call was terminated from the other end.

The agents looked at each other and knew this wasn't a good sign. They didn't even know there was a second ring set up! All of their missions were on a "need to know" basis and this one was obviously no different. Delta turned the key in the ignition, and at the same time Jerry's head spun around as he heard the car start. It reached them before they were both inside the coffee shop. He stopped mid-step and watched it as it zoomed past him and out of sight. His first impression was right. He was sure of it! The driver stared at him as he drove by. It was almost like slow motion going 80 miles per hour! He put the face to memory and ran up the few steps to join Eliza inside the shop to wait for the cab.

## Chapter 8

The ride to the morgue at Sunny Break Hospital, where the remains of Dorothy Stringer lay, took 45 minutes. Jerry spent most of the drive looking out the back window, but the blue sedan was not behind him and by the time they arrived at the hospital he was breathing a bit easier again, confident they hadn't been followed. He didn't know that cabs are easily traced, so the beige car two miles behind him knew exactly where they were going and wasn't going to risk being spotted.

The cab let them off at the emergency exit, and they walked inside the brick building. Shiny floors leapt up to greet them, along with a security guard. He was a permanent fixture just inside the front doors since a deadly flu-like virus outbreak months ago. The stern-faced guard stood up as they entered. The metal chair he was sitting on screeched backward on the scrubbed tile floor.

"Can I help you?" he asked pleasantly with a fake smile that never reached his eyes. He was paid too little and the shifts were too long to be honestly nice to people. He folded his arms and took a ready stance, which Jerry thought was a bit much.

"Yeah," Jerry answered.

"My friend here," he spoke as he laid his hand on Eliza's shoulder, "is expected at the morgue (a bit of a lie) to identify a friend who is recently deceased."

Eliza, who had been resting her head on the door jamb, turned her stark white face toward the guard, giving him her full attention. It didn't take a genius to see she had been through the emotional wringer not long ago, so instead of asking more questions, he asked them to disinfect their hands, put on slippers to cover their shoes, and wear gloves and a mask. He gave them directions to the morgue and wished them a good day, happily sinking back onto the metal chair and checking his watch. He saw his shift was almost over. Thank God!

They found the elevator easily enough and took it down six floors to the sub-basement. Morgues are always underground. So depressing, she thought. As if it isn't bad enough you have to come to see a dead body, you have to go to the bowels of the earth to do it!

They left the elevators and walked up to a brightly lit reception area. A masked nurse in a colourful blue, pink and yellow pantsuit stood up to greet them from behind a tall counter with a sliding window. Pushing aside the glass window, she said, "Yes? Can I help you?" in a quiet, muffled voice as if she was going to wake the dead.

"Hello," said Jerry, gesturing to his companion. "This is Eliza McPhelimy. She is here to identify the body of her friend, Dorothy Stringer."

Eliza stepped forward and showed her identification to the nurse, who looked down at her chart and then back up with a puzzled expression on her face.

"I'm sorry, but we don't have a Dorothy Stringer listed in the morgue. Are you sure she was brought here?"

"Yes! I'm sure. I mean…" he said, looking sideways at Eliza and raised his eyebrows, "we are sure!" Jerry responded.

Great, this was all they needed. Incompetence! He took a step away from the desk for a moment and flexed his shoulders to release the pent-up tension. He calmly walked back and asked, "Please check again," with more patience than he really felt.

"She died this morning. Her address is 4950 Warrant Terrace, North York. Police said it was suicide. She was brought here for the autopsy."

Eliza watched as the nurse re-checked her list, and when she met her eyes above the masks, she knew two things. One…that the nurse was going to deny Dorothy was here, and two…that she was definitely lying!

"I'm sorry, but we don't have a Dorothy Stringer listed. I would suggest you call the police and confirm what hospital she was taken to. If there is nothing else…" she asked, looking from one to the other, not really wanting them to respond. "Perhaps you could check with admissions?" she added cheerfully before closing the glass window and turning her back to them.

Eliza stood there for a moment trying to understand what was going on. She reached out and grabbed Jerry's hand and backed away toward the elevators. Jerry sensed a change in her and folded his fingers around hers and let himself be led away willingly.

Once the door of the elevator was shut, she dragged her white mask down to her chin and blew out a breath she didn't know she was holding. She turned to her young friend.

" She was lying!" she said, starting to pace the small space."I saw it in her eyes. I heard it in her voice. Now what? Where do we go from here?"

"Well," he said, "We could stake out the staff parking lot and follow her home. Perhaps away from prying eyes she may tell us the truth."

"Worth a shot," she agreed. "What I really need is a hot shower and some real food. Let's go to my apartment until she is off duty. It's not that far from here"

"One problem," he said wearily, running his hand through his hair again and rubbing the space between his eyes. "We have no idea when she gets off duty! Any ideas?" he said as he looked at her with raised brows.

"Come on! We're reporters, remember! We'll think of something!" She smiled and reached up to pull his earlobe.

They walked back to the security station and disrobed of their gowns, masks and shoe covers. They headed out of the hospital into the warm sunshine. It was now after 2 p.m. and the city was a hot pressure cooker. How she longed for the country. She grew up north of Orillia, a small city of 30,000 about an hour and half from the outskirts of Toronto. It was a slower pace there but in no way was it Hicksville. Instead of living there, though, she longed for the bright lights of the big city. She wasn't ready to shut down at 10 p.m. She loved the city that never slept. Their lights would now be irrevocably dimmed forever, as far as she was concerned.

This wasn't just another murder. This was the slaying of her best friend. How do people survive the death of their child, or losing their spouse or parents? She wondered and not for the first time! The only other casualty that had affected her so much that the paper took her off the file was the murder of a young child whose body had washed up off a tiny Toronto island last year. She knew she couldn't objectively do a good account. She had met the young girl while doing a story on her school's science contributions.

Two months later she was dead. The rage and grief she felt sent her to counseling and resulted in her taking a leave of absence for 6 months. Now that the trial was over and the killer sentenced to death, she finally slept at night. The best thing the government ever did was bring back the death penalty in 2007 and changed the laws so that if a criminal is convicted of murder and only sentenced to life…they spent their life in jail, not 25 years and out in twelve. Better yet, if sentenced to death, they died. End of story! Gone are the old rules. A criminal didn't just get a few years with time off for "good" behaviour. It was about time! Too many murderers killed again and again. There was no justice, just as there was no justice today! She grabbed her cell phone from her purse and dialed 411.

After receiving the phone number via a frustrating automatic attendant named "Myrtle," Eliza called Sunny Break Hospital and asked to speak to the administration department. Once there she pretended to be a cousin of the nurse whose nametag she had memorized, and said she had just arrived from Vancouver and wanted to surprise her cousin after work. The assistant was only too happy to help a fellow employee, and readily gave out the time she would get off shift.

Slamming her flip phone shut she said, "OK, we have until 7:45 tonight. That is when she is finished work. Let's get the hell out of here."

# Chapter 9

Mabus had seen the beige sedan sitting outside the hospital after he had followed the two reporters to the hospital. He still hadn't figured out who the beautiful young woman was with the guy from the Stringer house. It was only a matter of time he mused to himself. Only a matter of time!

He knew instinctively the guys in the car were spies. Spies he despised, he always said. They were part of the organizations that had tried several times in the past to find out who he was. Even when they did secretly discover what he looked like, he would just change his appearance and obtain new identities, so they would have to start at square one again. He had been relatively safe for a couple years now. He knew who they were, but they hadn't found him out yet.

He held back as the two young people were questioned by the weak excuse for a security guard. He heard them mention the morgue. Since he didn't need to go there, he retraced his steps and left the hospital to take care of the menaces outside.

Reaching inside his many hidden pockets in his overcoat, he withdrew the wires and plastics required for the job. The best part, he mused, with being a killer was the quick access he had to all the tools necessary for jobs that sprung up out of the blue. He was always prepared for the unexpected. He walked past the car on the opposite side of the street, watching the watchers out of the corner of his left eye. He could see they were staring intently at the exit door, so he walked up another half a block and then doubled back on the opposite side of the street.

"Man, this is my lucky day!" he said aloud to no one.

The car was parked next to a garbage Dumpster. At just that precise moment a city garbage truck had pulled up with all its noise and commotion. He ducked down between the car and the garbage truck and quickly placed the hastily prepared bomb in the tailpipe. As soon as these guys started the engine, the car and its occupants would cease to exist.

He was under the car and then standing on the other side of the street in less than two minutes. Happy and humming to himself, he walked briskly away to the next bus stop and hopping on, asking the driver it if went as far as Finches Avenue. After finding out that it did, he found a seat in the very back of the bus and fiddled with an unlit cigarette.

Damn rules, he thought to himself. No smoking on buses sucks!

The bus was only two blocks away when the enormous explosion took place. The driver pulled the bus over, much to Mabus's chagrin, and the people piled off in a rush to see what had happened.

Mabus didn't join the rush backward but instead strode ahead to the next subway station. He grabbed the first train northward to the edge of the city, where he knew his next victims waited for him. He smiled and hummed and nodded to bystanders who must have thought, Wow, a nice Torontonian! Go figure!

# Chapter 10

The two occupants in the beige sedan were listening in on the cell phone call and readily reported their findings to control. The orders were clear and concise, as if they were ordering a hamburger and fries. They were advised to intercept and terminate nurse at said time, before the couple planned to follow her at 7:45 that evening. Servicing would take place immediately after to erase any trace of them being there. The two men looked at each other and then out the front window of their car. Today was going to be another shitty day. Neither man liked killing a woman. But if it was to protect the innocent, then it was part of the job, and they accepted that. It was all for global security. They bought into this and fed on it like the ravenous carnivores they were. So, one more had to die. Hundreds of thousands already had. It is just that the blind public didn't realize it. It was their job to make sure they never did!

Echo was two years off retirement and Charlie was near the same. They were both middle-aged and single. Neither had married, and with little or no family, they were the perfect hybrids for the organization. They knew a lot more about this covert operation than the first setup. They knew the dangers and accepted their fate. They decided to drive around the block and get a better vantage point for when the target got off work. The driver turned the key in the ignition and the next moment a huge explosion blew the car and its occupants 50 feet into the air.

A mass of flaming debris came crashing down to the earth, scattering body parts and metal over the crowded streets below. Screaming people ran for cover as the flames ignited more cars and more explosions were heard. It looked like a war zone! Had full-scale terrorists finally erupted in Canada and launched the first of their attacks? It was the first thing on the minds of police and firemen as they raced to the scene. What met them was an unbelievable sight. Bodies lay in the streets, some burned beyond recognition. Burned out shells of several cars littered the streets and lawns of the huge, crowded hospital block.

Victims screamed in pain as doctors and nurses worked frantically to hurry them into the hospital. They all moved fast to contain the area and put out the fires. It was too late for 42 people, though. It was their first taste of battle on Canadian soil. The only positive thing was that it happened right outside the hospital building. Otherwise, more would have perished waiting for ambulances to arrive.

Eliza and Jerry, oblivious to what happened behind them, arrived at her apartment on Finches Avenue around 3 p.m. She dropped her purse and keys on the blue granite kitchen counter and reached inside the fridge for a bottle of water. After offering one to Jerry, she unscrewed the cap on hers and took a big swig before turning on the television. She used it more for noise than info, but as always it was tuned into Canadian News Net.

Jerry asked where the washroom was. She pointed without looking to the end of the hallway on the right. He left her in the living room to relax and watch the tube. He found it quickly and reached inside the darkened room to flick on the light. What greeted him surprised him. Her apartment was so trendy Toronto and yet her bathroom was 100 percent country. The walls were done in bright yellow and blue, and the border around it held birdhouses, cats and birds. An old birdhouse sat on one corner of the long vanity and the toilet paper holder was also in the shape of a birdhouse. He smiled as he looked around and thought to himself that this was more of the real Eliza then the one in the living room at the moment.

"Quick, Jer! Come here QUICK!" she yelled down the hallway.

He ran at breakneck speed to join her, but then she put a finger to her lips and motioned for him to watch the TV. When he heard her call out, is heart had skipped a beat. Maybe two!

For this? He thought to himself. A TV Show?

"Breaking news!" shouted the smiling news anchor from the wide-screen TV that took up much of her eastern living room wall. "Forty-two people confirmed dead in downtown Toronto. Some are speculating it was a terrorist attack. More details in a moment after this break."

Eliza quickly hit the mute button and grabbed the phone off its cradle. Instinctively she dialed the newspaper. She reached Ginny at the front desk. The young woman quickly advised her about what she knew and asked when she and Jerry were coming in. There was a rush meeting going on for all reporters. Eliza filled her in about quitting earlier that day and said she would tell Jerry about the meeting when she hung up.

"Holy shit! Can you believe this?" Eliza said as she turned to him and grabbed the front of his jacket. "We were just there! We were just there! We could have been killed, too!"

Jerry watched her as she turned white as a sheet and then she mumbled, "Oh my God, I think I am going to..." Jerry caught her as she floated toward to the floor and dragged her unconscious body to the nearby couch.

God! For a thin woman, she sure weighs a lot! he thought.

He wasn't really sure what to do next. He dug his hands into his hair and wanted to scream. Should I call 911? No! Two calls to them in one day might seem suspicious. Get a damp towel. Yes that's it! Revive her.

He continued talking to himself as he ran to the bathroom and dampened a towel and brought it back to the still unconscious Eliza. He wiped her face and arms and then held the towel to the back of her neck as she started to come around. His clear blue eyes met her wide green ones, and in an instant he wanted to kiss her. She was having no part of it, though, and putting a hand to his face, pushed him aside so that he fell with a thump onto the floor. She struggled to sit up.

"What are you doing? Did I faint?" she asked his prone

body as she raised herself up. Just as quickly, she swooned once more. Any thoughts of standing at the moment were put to rest, and she plunked her ass back onto the sofa.

"Yes, you did, and I was trying to revive you…you…idiot!"

It was the French tone to his accent that made her smile and then laugh. When she didn't stop, he knew she may be going into shock. Shutting his eyes, he swung back his hand and smacked her full in the face. When no sound other than the slap could be heard, he slowly opened one eye and then the other and watched as the shock fanned across her face and then the anger spots showed on her cheeks. Phew…she was back.

"Why, you jerk!" she exploded. "You-you pompous dumbass!" Then she leapt on him fists ready to pummel when as quickly as she wanted to tear him apart, realization set in. What was she doing? She lowered her fists, but not before giving him a quick jab in the gut and climbed off him, mumbling a contrite, "Thanks!"

"Anytime." He grimaced back and grabbed his bottle of water off the coffee table and took a large swallow.

They sat on the couch and listened to the news again as the anchor gave the latest details. The details both were sure had been "cleaned up" first. It had to be more than a coincidence that this "accident" happened at the same spot where they were asking questions.

"The nurse!" they both said in union. Eliza reached the phone first and called Sunny Break. She told the receptionist in clipped tones that she wanted to speak to Mrs. Clarke in the morgue. It was an emergency. After what seemed forever, and after hearing a series of clicks on the line, she came back on to say no one by that name worked there.

"What do you mean she doesn't work there? I spoke with her earlier today in the morgue!"

"I am sorry. But the person you are asking for does not work at Sunny Break," came the firm reply. "Are you sure you have the right name? We have so many Clarkes here. I did not catch your name? Miss?"

Eliza quickly hung up the phone and relayed the discussion to Jerry, who knew at once something beyond their scope of understanding was happening here. Just then the news anchor came back on the screen to announce the body count at 43. Another body of a woman yet unidentified had been found near the attack site. Looking at each other, they knew. Without further description, they knew. The body belonged to Mrs. Clarke.

## Chapter 11

The subway took no time at all to arrive, and Mabus swiftly boarded and found an empty compartment. He flipped open his cell phone and, using an online phone book, starting calling cab companies until he found the one that had picked up the two people from the hospital. He gave them a fake police badge number, and the dispatcher gave him the address they were delivered to. A half hour later he was standing outside the building, looking down the road at another telltale sedan parked with another two lackeys inside. "God!" he said aloud, "don't you guys have a job to go to?"

Mabus knew the men didn't see him. He stood now at the side entrance to the building and waited patiently, smoking a cigarette until someone would come through the door and let him in. It happens all the time. Don't people ever wonder how men like him get inside secure buildings and people end up dead? The human race is a race of really stupid people, he mused. Ten minutes later the steel door opened to let out an elderly lady dragging a steel shopping cart. The ever-helpful Mabus offered her his hand, and she readily accepted.

"My, but aren't you a nice man!" She smiled up at him. "My pleasure, ma'am," Mabus said and tipped his head while keeping one hand on the open door.

After wishing each other a good day, Mabus slipped inside and made his way to the front desk area where he knew he would have to find someone who knew who this girl was.

He didn't have to look very far. Seated in an old, lumpy armchair just inside the front foyer was an old man. He looked like he'd seen better days, and he smelled strongly of liquor. Mabus walked silently up to him and sat down in the chair opposite.

Nudging the old guy on the knee, he said, "Hey, old man, you gotta smoke?"

The old fella opened his eyes and looked blearily at what looked to him to be the long-dead actor Jules Brenner.

"Jules, is that you? I thought you were dead? I loved you in The Man from Malta."

Mabus realized right away this wasn't going to go well. The guy not only was a drunk but was delusional as well. He decided to play along.

"Thanks! That was quite some time ago, wasn't it? My death was exaggerated because I was sick of the press. Same as good ol' Elvis, too. You remember him? Great singer," he said as he helped the old guy sit up better in the chair.

"Yeah, that's right," the old man agreed. "It's good to see you, Jules. Alive, that is!" he said as he smiled a toothless grin.

"Listen, ah, what is your name?"

"Jimmy," Came the reply.

"Yeah, OK, Jimmy. I am supposed to meet my niece here."

"She's a pretty thing, long red hair, slim, great legs. Do you know if she is here yet?" Mabus asked as he leaned forward, putting one hand into his inside pocket.

"Oh yeah, sure buddy. I saw her with some young guy. Oh, her momma ain't gonna like that! She went straight up to her flat." He nodded as if somewhere in his mind he was having another conversation.

"Right, then," said Mabus. "Number 306, right?" This was just a guess.

"316," corrected Jimmy.

"Thanks, old buddy," said Mabus as he leaned forward to give the old man a one armed rapper hug and drove a long hypodermic needle into his heart.

So quick and skilled was the assassin that no sound was uttered by the old man and only a small pinprick of blood came through the front of his shirt. The poison would work quickly, almost instantly. If death could be painless, he considered this the most efficient way to make it happen. Mabus pulled the needle out and dropped it into his coat pocket. Pulled the old man's coat tighter around him and turned the body sideways in the chair so no one would suspect he was dead for a little while yet.

Giving the old man a small absent pat on the knee, for a brief moment he felt sorry for him without really understanding why. Then stood up straight and walked to the stairwell and climbed up three stories to stand outside room number 316. Checking out the lock, he knew it was going to be an easy one to pick.

# Chapter 12

"Why was she a threat, do you think?" Eliza asked Jerry as she hurriedly threw a few of her things into a travel bag. He had suggested they not stay at her apartment until they found out what was going on. Too many bodies were piling up too quickly. She had to agree.

"I think because she had contact with us. Me...you...I don't know. I am as confused as you are right now."

"But we know basically nothing! Except Dorothy had a mom who died the same way she did and obviously someone doesn't want us to know the truth. Could it be that if the truth were to come out it might have something to do with this lineage side of things, this Davidic line you spoke about?"

Outside listening ears suddenly pricked up!

"I think anything is possible at this point!" Jerry said as he turned up the volume on the TV set and put a finger to his lips. He grabbed her hand and led her to the bathroom.

"I saw this in a spy movie once," he whispered.

He turned on the shower and dragged both of them inside. God! The water was freezing, but it cleared their heads quickly. After reaching past him to turn the dial on the wall to adjust the temperature, she stood upright again and faced him. Once more, he put a finger to his lips to silence her when he knew she was to speak. He leaned down to touch his lips to hers. Before she could protest, he was kissing her. He was kissing her better than she had ever been kissed. If there was to be one famous kiss in all of mankind, this was it. She was literally floating! Her knees gave out on first contact, and he held her up against the glass shower door. Butterflies that hadn't existed since she was 15 rose out of nowhere and attacked her almost painfully. She opened her eyes a bit to watch him. His dark hair was dripping wet, matted against his tanned face. Long, impossible lashes fanned his cheeks as he reveled in the art of making kissing love to her. Kissing love, she thought. Ha! That's a new one. But it is like he is making love with his lips! So that is why so many get their tongues pierced. Mmmm...

She never wanted it to end, but knew it must.

Dragging her lips away from his, she stood there staring at him, breathing heavily and wanting to attack him. His arms had crept up around her at some point, and hers had entwined themselves behind his head. The water dripped off his nose and fell on her forehead. At 6 feet tall he was still 4 inches taller than she.

"We have to leave here, Eliza. It is not safe," he said as he pushed the hair back from her face and caressed her cheek with the back of his hand. "We don't know the whys, and it doesn't matter right now. I don't want us to get dead, to quote something from a movie."

" I can't be sure of anything right now, but your apartment might be bugged. I thought of that as we were watching the newscast and wondering if we were being followed earlier. Someone showed up at Willy's and raced away when I spotted them, and now Sunny Break hospital, too? There are ways to listen with a satellite link. Even see us standing here right now from above. Scary, isn't it? But in the spy movies sound cannot penetrate water, so until we know for sure this is where we talk, even in hotel rooms, OK?"

She nodded, still unable to speak much. Her lips were still trembling from the kiss.

"Grab only what you need. That means minimum clothes and women stuff and cash. Take out the pretty things I saw you stuff in there. You need practical jeans, shorts, a shirt and a jacket. We'll have to stop using our debit and credit cards since they are too easily traced. We'll have to make a stop at the bank or cash a cheque soon, as we won't have access for too much longer, I expect. Now when we turn the water off, we hum or talk about non-threatening things only, OK? Actually..." He thought as he tapped his index finger to his chin. "Why don't we divert the diverters?"

"What?"

"Follow my lead and agree to whatever I say, OK?" When she shrugged her shoulders and simply nodded, he turned off the water and reached outside the glass door to get her a towel.

She left him in the bathroom, as he said he wanted to have a real shower this time, and went to her bedroom to rummage around in her closet. She found some clothes the ex forgot to take with him when he left her last year, and she knew upon eyeballing them that they would fit Jerry better than they had fit what's-his-face. She went back into the bathroom and told him to throw his wet stuff in the tub and after he was finished showering his dry clothes would be on the vanity. God, he was a great kisser, she thought as she touched her fingers to her bottom lip, which was still tingling. I wonder what else he is great at she mused. Smiling to herself, Eliza walked back down the hallway to her bedroom and went back into the closet to retrieve her jacket. She felt rather than heard a presence behind her and, thinking it was Jerry, turned to face him with a grin that faded quickly. Her eyes grew wide as she stared at the stranger blocking the doorway behind her. He was tall, bald and dressed in what looked like an expensive suit. He smelled strongly of cigarette smoke, and he was aiming a silver gun right at her chest!

"So we meet at last, Miss McPhelimy," he sneered. His voice was so cold and creepy it made her shiver instantly. "I'm sorry I missed you at the hospital, so I did the next best thing and took out the suits that were casing you, plus a few more as a freebie!"

"That was you? You killed all those people? Why? How could you kill 43 people! And how the hell do you know my name?"

She spoke as loud as she could in her strangled voice, hoping Jerry would hear her over the shower water, which she could still hearing drumming into the tub. She was terrified! This can't be real! her mind kept screaming. There was no way to alert Jerry. He would be done with his shower soon and then he would walk into this killer's trap and they'd both be dead!
"Your name that part was easy. You left some mail on the counter. I simply just read it! And…yes, it was fantastic, wasn't it? I do so love the noise that a good bomb makes." He

was starting to sound a bit maniacal now, even to his own ears, so he said, "But enough about me. I want the journals."

"What journals?" she asked, too confused to be afraid at the moment.

"The journals your boyfriend took from the reporter's house. I saw him there. I was there."

It would only be a matter of time, seconds, before she and Jerry would join the list of the dead. Unless she could warn him somehow! But how could she do this? How; when a gun is aimed at her chest. It wasn't like she could disarm this maniac!

"You...you killed her, too?" She stammered. She had to keep him talking. Maybe Jerry would hear him and call the police or something!

"No...someone else beat me to it," he sighed as he shook his head. As if it was a shame.

When she was going to ask more questions, he put a black-gloved finger to his mouth to silence her. He motioned with the gun for her to go stand against the far wall of her room she moved slowly, doing as she was asked, still clutching a pair of panties. "Jerry!" her mind screamed, "hear me, Jerry! Don't come in here!"

She tried to mentally send him a message without having any way of knowing if was even receptive to that sort of thing.

"Eliza?"

"Answer him and sound normal, or else!" the gunman coldly said while waving the gun menacingly at her.

"Uh, yeah?" she answered as normally as possible. Her voice was slightly muffled from the bedroom.

"I think we should go to Niagara Falls. You know, get away from all of this. What do you think?"

When she didn't answer him right away, Jerry could sense the hairs on the back of his neck rise. She was too quiet. This was so not like her!

"Think! Think!" his mind screamed.

Something was wrong. Someone must be in there with her. Should he keep talking?

"Yes…keep talking!" his mind answered. He hurriedly looked around the bathroom for anything that might be deemed a weapon, while still rambling on out loud about where they would go and what they would do. Then his eyes spotted something. "Hmmm," he whispered, "what do we have here?"

He bent down beside the basin's cabinet. On the floor, standing up in a plastic bucket, was a wood-handled toilet bowl brush. He took judo lessons years before. Now, if his training didn't fail him, this could work.

He turned up the shower radio that was stuck to the back of the shower wall and then turned on the water in the bathroom sink. As an afterthought, he dumped her electric razor in the water without plugging it in. He then crept silently along the wall outside the bathroom, his steps muffled in the thick grey carpeting. He held the wooden stick at ready and peered through the crack in the bedroom door. He could see her just inside the crack of the bedroom door. His breathing was so loud and jerky he was sure people in the next apartment could hear him. His chest was tight from trying to stay calm. She was standing with her back against the wall on the far side of the bedroom. Her eyes were darting from the doorway to a spot behind the open door. So predictable...so Hollywood, he thought. But what a smart girl! She had just told him without saying a word that she wasn't alone.

OK, so we do have an intruder, and this person is hiding behind the door. A gun could be trained on her, and I have a stick! And...I have the shaver!

"Eliza, I need a shave. I'll be in the bathroom for a few minutes shaving, OK?" he called as he backed down the hallway.

A gut feeling had him diving inside the bathroom doorway just as the bedroom door crashed inward and a bullet whistled past his head. He had only moments to react before the gunman reached the doorway, so he took the razor out of the sink and threw it into the hallway. As if on cue, the killer stopped and, with a confused look on his face, picked up the shaver from the floor. At the same time Jerry plugged it in. The resulting surge knocked Jerry off his feet and sent him crashing into the shower door. The killer simply let out one strangled yell before he convulsed to the carpet. The man's gun had literally melted into his own hand. Jerry broke the shower door when he fell, but the plug held tight, and the other end fried the gunman until he literally smoked. Jerry got up and quickly jumped over the smoking dead guy and grabbed for Eliza, who was crouched on the floor near the bedroom door. Her arms hugged her knees as she sobbed.

"You okay?" he said with a high-pitched squeal that tilted

him toward madness himself.

"He...he said he wanted the journals!" she gasped. "What journals is he talking about, Jerry? He said you took them from Dorothy's apartment!"

"I didn't take any journals. I didn't see any!" he added quickly. "I took the story she was working on, put it in an envelope, and dropped it off at the front desk at work before I headed up to see you, but that was all."

"We have to get that envelope back now! Jerry, this is getting out of control!"

"Stay right here. I am going to take a couple steps back and see if this guy has ID, OK?"

When she simply nodded, not taking her eyes off the carpeted floor, he removed his hands from her arms and turned around.

He had never killed anyone before and what he really wanted to do was throw up. He fought down the nausea and went back down the hallway to bend over the stench that was once a man. He was a killer, he reminded himself. They were only defending themselves. He searched into the smoking pockets but couldn't find any ID on the man. That didn't surprise him! He did find several packs of smokes in every imaginable pocket, some wires, stuff that looked like child's play plaster, and a very expensive gold lighter. There was about five hundred in American paper bills and some coins. He took the paper money and turned back to Eliza.

"We're going to need this," he said, handing her the money. Upon seeing her questioning look at the wad of cash in his hand, he said, "He doesn't need it anymore. We've got to get to a phone booth and call the cops so someone can take this guy away. I have no idea how I am going to explain this one, except it was self-defense. But first we had better leave now!"

Jerry went back into the bathroom and hastily dressed in the borrowed clothes. Then they grabbed onto each other, picked up her bag, and fled the apartment.

Outside the apartment building, the blue sedan pressed back into service was listening to everything. The British spy movies were right, as for a time they could only hear the TV and water running.

"Shit!"

"What is that, D? Is that your favorite word of the day or what?"

"Yeah, sweet cheeks, it is!" He retorted sarcastically as X-ray tech chuckled. "They are running water up there, and I can't hear a damned thing. You think they actually know to do that in case someone is listening?"

His partner looked sideways at him and said, "What do you think? There have been enough movies produced by ex-CIA people to inform the whole world about most of our secrets. Come on… the real 007, the real Jackal, conspiracy theorists, enemy of the free world, and the list goes on. People think that stuff is made up when in actual fact it's more non-fiction than fiction. Of course, they could simply be having a shower together, in which case we'll know soon enough as you'll be hearing the moaning before too long!"

He laughed quietly at the thought and was sorely missing his live video hookup at this moment. With it he could be seeing inside the apartment right now. But control was afraid if they were spotted by CSIS that the equipment would be a dead giveaway. Just then the sound of a gunshot echoed in their ears.

"What the hell?" they both said in union and quickly jumped from the car and raced down the street toward Eliza's apartment building.

They pushed past an old couple just leaving the building and, amid curses and finger pointing, one ran to the stairs and the other to the elevator to get up to the third floor apartment that belonged to Eliza.

Delta reached it first by taking the stairs, and he stood out of breath in front of door 316. Within 30 seconds X-ray ran out of the elevator and together they placed one kick to the door and it fell in.

"God! What is that stench?" choked D as he quickly covered his mouth with the arm of his suit jacket.

They quickly searched the rooms one by one with guns drawn and at the ready. It didn't take long to locate what they were looking for. X-ray bent down and rested his gun on his thigh as he did a quick pulse check.

"Dead," he said as he holstered his gun. "Looks like the shaver fried him. Pretty quick thinking, if you ask me. You know who he is?"

Delta knelt down beside his partner and took a good look at the blackened face. File pictures flashed across his brain.

"I can't be sure, but he looks like a guy named Mabus! He was a rogue spy from overseas! I've only ever seen one picture of him, and I can't be sure. Dental records will confirm for us who he is. I just can't be sure, as this guy Mabus is like the Jackal and changes his identity with the weather. Better radio in to control and tell them what we've found. I'm going to check around to see what I can find."

He left X-ray to call the kill in and did a quick search of Eliza's apartment. He found her computer tucked away under the bed and did a quick scan of its hard drive. Nothing! Why are these two involved in this mess? he asked himself. He still didn't see a link and wondered if they were actually their protectors and not their eliminators! They needed answers and now! This covert just didn't add up!

"They've called in the cleaners. They should be here shortly," said X-ray as he walked over to the living room window and looked out. "What do you make of this, D?" he asked as he turned around to face his partner.

"I don't know," He shook his head with a perplexed look on his weathered face. "I think we need some answers, buddy. These two kids don't seem to have any real connection to Dorothy, who we knew had hidden state secrets. It was her threat to go to the media, her field of expertise that resulted in her demise. Let's just hope old Mabus here, if it's really him, was working alone. It doesn't look like he found anything either except an untimely end, which is good for us, as it means we won't have to do it ourselves."

They waited thirty minutes for the knock on the door and let the cleaners in. They would quickly dispose of the body after control had identified it, of course. The agents really didn't know exactly how they did it, and they never asked. It was better not to know and, therefore, never able to reveal any secrets under torture.

It worked for them! With one more look back at the body bag, they left the apartment as quickly as they could to meet with their covert director at a ritzy hotel in downtown Toronto. Too much time had passed now to go chasing through Toronto streets looking for these two. They had enough resources that it would only be a matter of time before the ring would pick them up and it would start all over again.

# Chapter 13

Eliza and Jerry took the service elevator to the bottom floor of her building. Jerry stole a glance outside the heavy doors to view through a side foyer window before they left. He didn't see the old man slumped in the chair, but he did immediately see two guys jump out of the blue sedan parked up the street. He grabbed Eliza's hand as they fled out the back entrance to the alley beyond. One man he was sure was the guy he recognized from that morning at Willy's.

They ran together to the end of the alley toward Birchmere Street and crossed over toward the subway entrance, running down the steps, and pushing passengers and shoppers out of their way in their haste. She threw the coins in the slot and they jumped over the turnstiles. They scrambled down more steps, taking them two at a time, to the subway platform below.

"Which one do we choose? Where do we go?" she asked as she frantically paced and looked up and down the subway line, trying to decide. "Do we go left or right?"

When he didn't answer, she stopped mid-step and asked him again.

"Jerry?" she said, putting her hands on her hips for effect. "Which way?"

He looked at her, but he was so intently studying the overhead subway system charts that he didn't hear her.

"Um, sorry! We need to find a safe place, I guess," he said as he caught her hand in his. "Someone not connected to you or me. Family or friend-wise, I mean. We need to go to Willy's!"

"Willy's? The coffee house Willys, you mean? Why there? It's not safe, Jer, those guys saw us there this morning. They are bound to go back, don't you think?"

"Yeah. Right guy. Wrong place, though. He isn't there right now. He's moved back up to his home village of Rama for a while. We can stay with him. We just have to get there. We'll take the subway to Yorkdale and then the GO train to Barrie. From there we can get a bus to Rama. We can probably ride on the casino bus for free!" he added as she looked at him. Her arms were crossed and a crease was showing between her brows.

"Don't frown," he said, "you'll get wrinkles!" He tugged at her hand to steer her toward the platform as the train was arriving.

"Creep!" she countered, and wrapped her fingers around his. They felt so good. So warm, so safe. It was a place she hadn't been to lately, and right now she didn't want it to end. Her body was still quaking from the scene back at the apartment. Now was not the time to dwell on it, though. They had to stay focused. Stay focused or they would die! This she was sure of.

"Fine!" she agreed, looking up into his face. "Let's just get going somewhere, OK? I don't relish being here, standing around in the open. I hate the subway at the best of times. It's an open spot for any crazy person who hates his or her ex to push some unsuspecting person in front of a train to ease his guilt for murdering them."

She removed her hand from his and rubbed them up and down her arms as she began to pace in a circle.

He watched her as she wore a path and finally said, "God! You really are a conspiracy theorist, aren't you! You don't trust anyone or anything!"

"Actually, Jer," she said looking up at him without missing a step, "I used to be that way, well for the most part at least"

They had a couple of minutes to kill before the next trains arrived, so she filled it by giving him her version of how she saw the world.

"I've always mistrusted governments," she stated. "Not just our own clowns but global governments as well. I hate the way they waste billions while millions of people starve, throw good taxpayers' money away on crap while making some old farmer register his old shotguns. Give me a break! The real thugs drive around in blue sedans with their guns strapped to their sides. And don't look surprised. I saw them parked outside my apartment before you did! Why are they following us? What did we do? Why are people trying to kill us?"

Seeing that her raised voice was bringing unwelcome stares from others waiting for the rain, she stopped speaking and kept quiet, but gave Jerry a look that demanded an answer anyway.

"No idea, Eliza. If I knew that, perhaps there would have been a way to avoid what has happened to us so far. But since I don't, let's get on this train," he said as they stood in line for the next train approaching. He continued, "And hopefully we haven't been followed. I have a gut feeling, though, that they aren't that far behind that they can't figure out where we were headed. We'll have to find out about the story Dorothy was writing later. It isn't safe for us to stay in Toronto any longer. We have to get out of the city!"

They boarded the train along with about 300 others and tried to melt into the crowd. Jerry's eyes never stopped searching, and three times they switched trains. One backtracked and two went forward. When they finally hit Yorkdale it was almost 8 o'clock and they nearly missed the last GO train to Barrie. The train was giving it's last warning whistle when they hopped onboard, the doors squeezing shut behind them.

"We forgot to get more cash Jer!" she said as they settled into the back seat of the end car. "I only have about a hundred bucks on me. How much do you have?" Jerry pulled out his wallet and counted a hundred and eighty and some pocket change.

"We have enough for today and tomorrow. Maybe a third day if we are careful. We have buses to pay for and maybe hotel. We'll see." He put the money back in his wallet and, turning to her, he smiled and said, "Oh yeah, and don't forget I have that five hundred American buckaroos from the dead guy!"

"I wish you wouldn't have taken that guy's cash. It just doesn't feel right."

Jerry ran his hand down her arm in a comforting gesture.

"Well, it's not like he's going to need it, right?"

He loved touching her even it was in a non-sexual way. Lost in his thoughts, her question made him simply stare at her for a moment. Lost in his emotions, his tongue simply couldn't find words until she asked him again.

"What is it about you French guys?" she asked. His eyes creased at the sides as he replied.

"What do you mean by 'French' guys?"

"Oh, I don't know," she responded, and then added, "You have a way of making everything seem right. Hah, must be your accent!" She laughed. "Nah," he said, "more like we are fearless men who love to protect little women like you."

"Why, you pompous ass!" she said as she punched him in the arm.

"Ow! Hey! What did I do to deserve that?" He laughed as he rubbed his new sore spot.

She tilted her head and sat forward so that her body was angled toward his and, leaning toward him, looked straight into his eyes as her hand grabbed onto his nuts and gave a good squeeze.

"Ayeeah! OK! OK ! I see! I see! Let go, you witch! You can take care of yourself. Now let go!" he cried while trying to drag her hands away from his cojones.

"That's better," she said, and released him. "And while we are at it. Yes, I am a witch. Here…see this?" She showed him her pentagram necklace she kept tucked inside her blouse

"Wow! A pentagram. So you are into that witch stuff, are you? Why didn't you just zap the bad guys then? But no! Let me expend my energies while you sit on the sidelines! You almost got me killed!" He was laughing now, trying to lighten the mood, and lightly fingered the Celtic silver pentagram.

"Because, you misinformed man person…we don't zap! I wish we could!" she said as she settled back into her seat again, still fingering the pentagram between her slim fingers.

"Although I wish I had that power, it's a nature-based religion. We use the power of the three and the universe to change things. And if I had had time to think or prepare today, I would have sent the wrath of Hecate on him." Seeing his quizzical look, she asked, "Why do you want to know any of this?"

"Sure, we have time. Why not." He countered.

"I have to know why, or I won't say. The four rules of a witch are to dare, to know, to will and to be silent. Therefore, I cannot tell you anything unless you have a really good reason for wanting to know!"

"OK." He nodded. "Let's just say I am not religious, but I am curious. Good enough for now?"

Eliza studied him for a long time before answering. He was probably just being polite, and she was grateful for the distraction.

"All right. But just so you know, I don't press my beliefs on anyone."

"Uh huh. Go on," he prompted.

"You want to know about Hecate, then to start off?"

"Yes, I do!" he said as the folded his fingers together over his stomach and leaned back against the seat. This all seemed so natural to him. So right, somehow!

So she began. "OK, Hecate is the Goddess of the Underworld. Nothing Satanic, but more of a protector of witches, or even you, if you needed it! If you are wronged, you say the Chant of Hecate and she rights things rather quickly in your favour. You just have to be sure you have no part in whatever you wanted to make right, otherwise it'll come back on you, too. And believe me you don't want that to happen!"

"Fascinating," he responded. He sat forward again and grabbed her hand, rubbing it gently in a circular motion that almost made her slide out of her seat in ecstasy. Putting on a brave face, though, she let him continue with his questions.

"So, you are telling me that even though I don't call myself a Pagan or witch or whatever, I can call upon this Goddess, or any other if I wish to? Cool!"

"Well, why not?" she countered.

"That's what I asked you!"

They chatted all the way to Barrie about Wicca and Witchcraft. She gave up trying to explain to him the difference between the two of them. She told him she was a hereditary witch, meaning her mother and her mother's mother and so on back at least five centuries had been witches. They preferred the term "wise one" to "witch," as it was deadly to admit you were one in the fifteenth to seventeenth centuries.

She was amazed that there were still so many misconceptions out there about it. He was more intelligent than she would have ever guessed. He asked logical, thought-provoking questions that even she herself had never pondered. He was an agnostic but had studied religion at school. He was astounded that so many untruths were still being taught.

When he asked to know more, she went through the basics with him, Wicca 101, if you will. It couldn't hurt, if she needed help later on, to tap into his natural energies.

The city lights of Barrie come into view approximately an hour later. They spanned out over both sides of the great highway. Their pinkish lights cast arcs into the sky overhead. It was wonderful riding the train in for a change. She usually drove past Barrie on her way to her parent's house in Orillia in a rental car, never stopping to enjoy the view of Lake Simcoe or Lake Couchiching. Especially lovely was downtown by Kempenfelt Bay with its waterfront trails and beautifully maintained parks. Orillia, too, had its own beautifully tended parks and boarded walkways along the waterfront.

It was dark when they arrived at the train station in Barrie, and after leaving the coach they decided to take a walk along the water's edge that was now lit with what appeared to be a thousand candles, but were actually streetlights. The reflections were illuminating the water. In their eyes it was simply breathtaking. They stood there, Jerry's arm draped casually around her shoulder, and watched as the waves lapped in upon the slightly rocky shore. Just off to their left sat a blue heron on one of the many limestone rocks that dotted both sides of the wooden boardwalk. Soundlessly, he lifted off. The bird's wide wings lifted him gracefully from the end of the pier. Watching in awe, they saw the weightless wings lift up and down in a mesmerizing pattern until it became a spec as it soared off in the distance. Looking back at each other and feeling the magic of the moment, he leaned down and gave her a quick kiss on her soft mouth. Without another word they both pulled back and continued to walk around the rest of the pier.

After their quick stroll had ended, they decided to grab a drink at the nearby Queen's Hotel and arrange a ride to Orillia before it got too late. They had been informed by the ticket person at the train terminal that the last connecting bus to Orillia left a half hour before they arrived. After getting seated, the waiter took their order and just as quickly delivered sumptuous morsels for them to eat, washed down with chilled beers.

"What are you going to do for clothes?" she asked between bites of potato skins and chicken wings. "We weren't able to stop at your place before grabbing the GO here!"

He looked sideways at her as he sipped his beer. They sat beside each other in the end booth at the bar, facing the front door.

"I could always borrow some of yours!" he teased.

When she didn't take the bait, he squinted at her, searching her face for any clue as to why this explosive character he loved did rise to an obvious tease. It wasn't like her. What he saw melted his heart. She looked exhausted. It was probably the food keeping her vertical, so he suggested after they finished eating that they get a room at the hotel. They could just as easily continue to Orillia and then up to Rama tomorrow. It made sense. They had more than enough cash to pay for the room.

Tomorrow he would do some shopping, call the office, and hopefully find time to do some research into what linked Dorothy, some missing journals, a nurse, Dorothy's mom, a movie star, a dead prime minister, and, of course, the idea that this had something to do with the lineage of Jesus and was somehow connected with them!

After finishing the quick bite at the bar they went to the front desk and registered under a fictitious name and dragged themselves and her backpack up to the second-story room.

The door key worked on the first try, which was amazing, as most keyless entries are anything but easy! The door opened to reveal a homey little room. There was a sitting area and a sunken bedroom to the right. A bright bathroom was to the left of the door, and a table and two chairs sat by the window.

Eliza went first to the window and glanced out. She saw nothing out of the ordinary, no dark sedans, no men in darks suits. Not that she could really see them in the dark anyway, but just saying so inside made her feel safer. She pulled the window shade down and flopped down on the bed. As her body sunk into the soft mattress, she groaned and thought she could sleep for six months.

When she had awakened that morning, it was like any other day. She got up, showered, got dressed, and got a cab to work downtown. She loved it. She would spend her lunches with friends. Most of the time was spent with Dorothy, though. As she thought of her friend, tears pricked the backs of her eyelids, threatening to spill forth one more time. She put her arm across her eyes and gave in, letting the tears fall where they may.

Jerry give the impression of being busy putting their things away and checking out the bar fridge. When he did steal a look over at her from where he was standing near the TV console unit, he saw the tears begin to form. Without warning, she began to sob. Her body convulsing as it was wracked by emotions so strong she felt it would crush her. He knew he had to let her cry it out. She hadn't had a chance today. It was too nuts. Their lives were in danger. It was crazy, like watching a Hollywood movie play out, and you could guess the ending. Except this time it was for real and the ending of this particular movie was nowhere in sight. He had to find a sterile phone and get in touch with the office and Willy soon. God, he was in a Hollywood movie!

In the meantime, he needed to get word to Willy through a connection in Rama, as Willy lived out in the bush with no phone or electricity. Just the way he liked it, he always said. He was probably the only person living in Canada who still rejected hydro and running water. There was so much to do, so much to find out, and whether she liked it or not, he was going to protect her. She wasn't as tough as she wanted him to believe.

Her sniffs brought his head back to look at her. He had been peeking around the pulled shade. There weren't any cars that hadn't been there when they arrived. Whoever was chasing them would know her parents lived in Orillia, or would find out soon. They were dealing with professionals here. He assumed that nurse, Mrs….somebody. God, he couldn't even remember her name! She had died because she told them a lie and they had figured it out. If we hadn't talked on the cell phone and said we would come back and follow her, she might still be alive; he thought Her death played heavily on him. He felt worse still because all he could remember is that the news anchor called her "victim number 43."

He walked over and sat on the edge of the bed. She was still sniffing, but she was fast asleep, so he pulled off her shoes and pulled up the comforter from the bottom of the bed and tucked it in around her slim body He then lay down, wrapped his arms around her, and fell into his own exhausted sleep. The next day dawned overcast and wet. The forecast was calling for rain for the next three days. He got up quickly from the bed, dressed and quietly left the room. He had things to do, and he might as well do them solo. She needed the rest anyway, and he knew he could get more accomplished when only one person was playing dodge ball with who knows who!

Jerry called the police from the first phone booth he came to on Dunlop Street, a block from the hotel, to report the death of the man in Eliza's apartment. When they wanted his name, he hung up. He had a sense she wouldn't be going back there anyway, so why give more details then they needed? It would only complicate things more than they already were. Then he called into work from a phone booth in the Georgian Mall at the far north end of the city, on Bayfield Street. He asked about the envelope he dropped off and, after checking around, he was told some police detectives had picked it up shortly after he left it at reception. It didn't come as a huge surprise. He would probably never know now what she was writing when she was killed!

He then told them he was taking an unexpected vacation to see his family in Montreal should anyone come asking, and then he took a cab back downtown to Dunlop street to buy some clothes and get some more cash from an insta-bank. He knew it would be a short matter of time before the cash would be traced, so he took another cab back to the top end of Barrie to the mall district and withdrew more cash there. He had the cabbie take him to Molson Park Drive, where all the huge stores were and he could spend lots of cash quickly. Finally, one last time, he withdrew more funds as far away from the hotel as was possible.

He had been gone nearly three hours by the time Eliza woke up. She got up, showered and dressed and was happy the room came with a self-service coffee maker. She made coffee, called room service, and placed an order of cream cheese, bagels and toast. She then sat down to read the complementary newspaper left outside their door. As swiftly as she picked the paper up, she set it back down and began to pace.

"Where the hell is he?" she asked herself. The delivered food in front of her was quickly forgotten after a few small bites. Pacing was the only thing she could focus on, and she lifted the window shade to take a peek outside! She had done it a million times at least by now, she thought. What was once more? Eventually she gave up pacing the room, and stood impatiently looking out the corner of the window from behind the shade. Cars and people came and went. No one in suits showed up, but Jerry wasn't anywhere to be found either! She guessed he had gone in search of clothes, but that must have been hours ago! Checkout time for the room was 11 a.m. and it was now 10:30. He had 30 minutes to show up before she would be on the street and vulnerable. Suddenly she heard the door handle click, and instinct drove her down behind the bed. Why? It seemed the logical thing to do, that's why!

Jerry came into the room carrying bags under his arms, and after depositing them near the bathroom door, he looked around, wondering where she had gotten to. For a moment his insides burned in panic, until he saw her hair peek over the top edge of the bed.

"It's me, Eliza. It's OK, you can get up now. You are safe," he whispered as he went to her and slowly squatted down in front of her as she sat on the floor.

Her head was on her knees, and she was trembling. Without hesitation he reached out and pulled her into his arms. Before he knew it, he was kissing her again. God, it felt good to kiss her. Her moans of pleasure urged him on and within moments all their clothes lay in a heap on the floor and they were making wild, passionate love on the floor. It was urgent and hot! Both of them were panting when it was over. He looked down at her as she looked up, and they smiled in unison.

"Well, I guess we've taken the step beyond friends and colleagues now, hmm?" she shyly asked.

In reply he bent down and began kissing her again. They started to make love again. They were slower this time, while relishing each other's bodies and taking the time to explore, tease and fulfill each other's needs that were spent too quickly before.

# Chapter 14

They checked out of the room a few minutes after eleven and walked down to the front desk to turn in their passkeys. The foyer was empty save an old couple sitting in the corner who looked like they, too, had slept in their clothes. Jerry was eyeing them strangely when the front desk clerk nodded toward them and said they were regulars who usually drank too much and ended up sleeping it off about once a week in that very spot.

They looked at the couple and wondered if anyone was missing them? They felt so alone except for each other at that moment. She couldn't see her family and neither could he! They couldn't call any friends other than Willy. To do so may bring them harm, or worse!

The desk clerk provided them with a bus schedule and a map, which they really didn't need, but didn't want to alert anyone that they knew where they were going. As far as the clerk knew, they were simple tourists. They left the hotel and walked the six blocks to the bus terminal to purchase their tickets. It would be a 25-minute wait, so they went across the street to the coffee shop and relaxed while they waited for the bus to arrive and load. They picked a table next to the outside wall with a window that had an excellent view of the train station. While they sipped their coffee, Jerry told her about calling the cops and about the conversation he had with reception at work about the missing story Dorothy was working on.

"That part will be a dead end now. We'll probably never know what she was working on."

"Did you ask if any journals were found?" she asked him inquiringly.

"Yeah, I did, and no, they didn't find any. Some detectives picked up whatever I left there. They didn't get their names or badge numbers. So we can only presume they weren't cops."

She nodded her head in agreement, and he went on.

"I also managed to get a message to Willy. He will be meeting us at the train depot in Washago," he said as he swallowed his coffee and munched on their new flavour of donut, maple cream with chunks of apples inside.

"Why Washago?" she asked, her facing screwing into a frown. "I thought we were going to Orillia?" She reached forward and grabbed a piece of his donut and jammed it into her mouth. She hadn't eaten much of the breakfast she had ordered earlier and was starving now!

"Because… if we are being followed, and I know we are or will be again shortly, they will think we will stop there. They are probably already staking out your parent's house. Instead, we'll continue on past Orillia and get off 20 minutes later. Hopefully it will throw them off our trail long enough for Willy to pick us up, and we can disappear for a few days. I wasn't able to do any more research while I was out. I was spending too much time going from one cash machine to another and hailing cabs!"

She nodded that it made sense and, looking thoughtful, she drank her own coffee in silence. No mention was made of this early morning romp. Neither of them, she believed, needed to discuss it. A new bond had formed between the two of them. He was almost eight years younger than her, but he was more mature than her ex, who had been eight years older. They clicked. She liked his French accent, his look and his intelligence. He was, in essence, what she needed, even though she gave up looking for it long ago. They saw the tall bus pull into the parking lot across the street and, knowing that was their cue, picked up their things and left the bustling coffee shop. There were only a few people on the bus, so they went to the back and relaxed in the overstuffed, high-backed seats.

The trip to Orillia was uneventful. No other stops were made on the way, and so they enjoyed the view floating by their windows. They watched farmlands flash by along with new subdivisions that had been popping up all over from Barrie to Orillia in the last few years. There was no reason to go to the big cities anymore. Everything you could possibly need was now coming to the smaller cities like Orillia. In addition to the retail outlets, they had a booming theatre district. A great many writers had emerged from the small city. Locals loved to boast that is was the home of famed author Stephen Leacock and equally famous and still living singer/songwriter Gordon Lightfoot.

They were told upon arrival that the next bus would leave for Rama and Washago in about three hours, so they stowed their gear in a locker and headed up Front Street to look at the local shops. She took him to her favourites, Mantacore Books, Season of the Mystic and The Mariposa Market, where he couldn't help but buy himself a Texas-sized donut. They looked around the music stores and then walked back down Mississaga Street to the lakeshore. The wooden boardwalks were busy with vacationers and locals. Some were fishing off the town dock while others were busy fussing with their big fancy boats. All in all, it was a lovely afternoon and they strolled back, hand in hand, to the bus terminal, eating chocolate peanut butter ice-cream cones they picked up at the Orillia Bakery.

They still had fifteen minutes to spare.

The driver let them on the bus early so they could sit in comfort while waiting for any last-minute arrivals. Soon they went up Front Street and then travelled across town on Laclie Street to meet up with Highway 11 at the north end of the city. The highway would take them directly to the small village of Washago. Eliza thought that she didn't believe Washago would stay small too much longer. A huge casino had been built on reserve land a number of years ago and was raking in millions every day. That money, or some of it, was funneled back into the native community (after the government took their share first, of course!) and new homes and businesses were springing up everywhere. But at what cost, she thought. Too many had become addicted to gambling. She knew, being a reporter, that too many lost homes, family and their lives. She had been working on this story the day before all hell broke loose!

The bus stopped in Washago fifteen minutes later on a rough, graveled parking lot close to the docks of Lake Couchiching. The other passengers must have been travelling on, as Eliza and Jerry were the only two to get off the bus. Waiting for them beside a new bright blue Dodge Ram truck was an old man. By his age and demeanor, Eliza guessed he must be the mysterious Willy. He reminded her of actor Graham Greene. Long grey-white hair, pulled back into a ponytail, fell almost to his waist. He had smooth skin on his face, except for a few wrinkles, and he had a sexiness she couldn't put her finger on. He looked great in those faded jeans! He pushed himself away from the truck when he saw Jerry, his hand outstretched.

"Hey, old dude! How the hell have you been?" said Jerry as he grasped the old man's hand in a firm shake.

"Hey, young creep! Damn good! Damn good!" he gave them both a huge smile that revealed the whitest teeth Eliza had ever seen. "You are also doing well, I see!" he said, winking at Eliza. "Nice lookin' woman you got there! Holding out on ol' Willy, eh?"

She felt a flush come right up from her ankles to turn her face crimson, and she prayed neither man saw it. It was embarrassing to blush at her age when a man who could be old enough to be her grandfather made a simple pass at her.

They threw their gear in the back of his pickup and headed out of the small village to Oak Ridges Road, where Willy kept his private cottage. The ride took about fifteen minutes, which gave them some time to become comfortable with each other. It had been a couple of years since Jerry and Willy last saw each other, and they spent the short drive laughing and trading barbs back and forth. It was a welcome respite to the ordeal they had just come through. When they rounded a bend in the road, Jerry sucked in his breath and said, "Holy shit, Willy! What have you done to the place?"

"Oh, a little of this, a little of that." He chuckled.

Eliza saw more than a little. His "little" cottage, as he called it, was huge! A three-story, three-tiered deck stretched up and around and out of sight as the cedar-sided home rose and fell in different sizes, shapes and levels. The glass on some of the windows must have been 30 feet high! Willy pulled his truck up to a three-bay garage and they all climbed out. Jerry's mouth was still agape when they walked up the first set of steps up onto the main deck.

Seeing their looks of awe, he said, "I got lucky at the casino." A little more than luck, Eliza thought to herself.

## Chapter 15

"Just so you know, young creep," Willy said jokingly, "I now have hydro and water. Made no sense to do without 'em after the hot tub was invented! And how would I keep my pool heated?"

"You have a pool?" asked Jerry incredulously.

The old man just laughed as opened the front door and led them inside the cavernous living room with an open concept loft area above. The walls and ceiling were done in knotty pine and three huge ceiling fans hung down in a row. He led them through the living room down three steps into a room with a lowered ceiling that Eliza knew was a gourmet's kitchen. Willy explained that he liked to cook and now entertained quit a bit. He said having all this space made sense. Without stopping, he took them up another flight of stairs to a separate hallway that had several doors leading off both sides.

"One room or two?" he asked as he looked from one to the other. "One," said Jerry

"Two," said Eliza. Both spoke their reply at the once.

They looked at each other dumbfounded and then back at Willy. "Well, when you guys make up your minds, you decide. For now, drop your stuff somewhere and join me downstairs. You can tell me why you called up old Willy to help you out." With that said he turned away from them and headed back down the same way he came, his moccasin-covered feet stepping noiselessly on the wood floors.

Eliza walked into the first room on her right and marveled at the decor. The bed was a huge, oversized wooden canopy. The posts had to be a foot in diameter each! The bedding was native in design and everything matched. The carpet was grey, lush and thick and made you want to curl your toes into it. She set her bag on the dark green velvet settee and walked to the large patio doors, which led to a private deck outside. She opened the doors and inhaled the fresh air. Nothing was like the air up here, she mused. She loved the scents that wafted through the air after a day's rain. The tangy perfume never left you no matter how long you'd been away from it. Not much changed around here either. The weather was always predicted wrong and off in the distance normalcy abounded as she heard someone cutting their grass while a floatplane roared overhead. Tipping her head back, she watched as it circled to land at a nearby runway. At the same time, she could hear the crickets in the nearby forest.

"This place looks like something out of Better Homes & Gardens magazine! I thought he was the last native without hydro and water?" she asked as she stepped back inside the bedroom.

"Yeah, so did I!" said Jerry as he tested out the mattress on the bed. "Very nice! Anyway, it appears the conveniences far outweigh the inconveniences of life now for him, and who can blame him? He probably never had much money in his life. The shop in the city never made him rich. Since Bill took over it's been more lucrative since he doesn't give it all away. Then the casino came to town, and band members all get cash from it. Why not spend it? I would! Hell, it makes me wish I had native blood running through my French veins.

Being French hasn't made me rich and probably never ill."

She had to agree with him. Not about the French part, but about being native and finally being able to take control of your life financially. To have this kind of home in Lake Country was a paradise. She just hoped it wouldn't be located for a few days so she and Jerry could find out why their lives were in danger. She silently hoped it wouldn't end up costing Willy his life. She guessed if something happened to him, a band of brothers would be quick to track the bastards that did it. That in itself brought her a small measure of comfort in an otherwise gloomy outlook.

She started to walk out the door to join Willy downstairs when she turned and said, "Just so you know, this is my room." She then sauntered out the door. "Ha! That is what you think!" he joked and, bounding off the bed, quickly followed her down the stairs.

Willy made them a dinner to remember. Fresh venison, grilled to perfection on his huge indoor barbecue, fresh green beans, a type of native bread with local freshly churned butter on it, and red-skinned potatoes.

"The only kind I buy," Willy said with a laugh, and they all joined in on the pun. Sated and sitting in overstuffed leather chairs placed around a huge double-sided fireplace, which he lit with a remote, they drank coffee and chatted into the wee hours of the morning. By the time they had filled him in as much as they could remember, he had gone silent. Still nodding his head as though they were still speaking to him, he stood up. Then, without another word to them, he went out of the room, exiting to still another set of stairs that led upward in the opposite direction, and didn't return.

They waited for about a half hour before realizing he wasn't coming back, and they went to bed as well. Looking at each other, they shrugged their shoulders and, holding hands as they went up the stairs, they went into the same room without saying anything to each other. They undressed quickly and climbed into the princess-like bed, curling into each other, and fell instantly asleep.

Eliza rolled over in the huge bed the next morning and reached out for Jerry. She realized the other side of the mattress was empty again. What was it with that guy? Did he ever sleep in?

She could tell by the direction of the sun outside the patio doors that it was at least mid-morning, and she scrambled out of bed to find Jerry and Willy. Dressing quickly in jeans and a t-shirt, she found her socks and forced her feet into her running shoes without untying the laces and went quickly down the beautiful, shiny wooden staircase.

All was quiet in the house as she descended. They must be outside somewhere, she mused. It was a good a chance as any to explore a bit of this enormous house. The kitchen was pristine. The sun glinted off the white porcelain and stainless steel. You'd never know if someone had made a cup of coffee there this morning. All of the appliances were the latest editions and, to her delight, built in. The fridge was made to look like a cabinet so that when you opened the cabinet door you were right inside the fridge. Very ingenious, she thought! She opened up cupboard doors and found the place well stocked in canned goods and all manner of cooking utensils. This was an organized man! She thought.

She went up the steps to the living room and ran her hands along the deep green leather sofas. The room must be 60 feet long, she thought, amazed at how homey it felt despite its size. The colour scheme was done in green and terracotta. A designers dream room, she thought. Sure beat the hell out of her white and silver decorated apartment! If she ever went back there, changes were going to be made, that was for sure.

The far end of the room held all types of electronic equipment. Two huge 52-inch screens were set in the walls, along with DVD players, CD players and stereo equipment that would rival any DJ's stuff. He also had two built-in computer terminals.

"Who is this guy?" she wondered aloud. This was no ordinary native retiree. She turned around toward the door as voices could be heard now from outside. Before her fingers touched the brass door handle, the door swung inward toward her, and Willy and Jerry marched in so quickly they nearly knocked her off her feet!

"Sorry, little lady! Didn't see you there!" said Willy as he put a steadying hand on her shoulder and moved her backward into the living room so he and Jerry could step inside and close the door behind them. They both held a popular breakfast restaurant's take-out bags in their hands, and the smells wafting out made her mouth water.

"Um, sure no problem, Willy. I was just admiring your, uh…stuff there!" she said as she pointed to the electronics wall.

"Yeah pretty cool, eh? Come with us! We've got breakfast. You hungry?"

Without waiting for her to respond, he and Jerry went down into the kitchen and sat down at the huge harvest table just off the cooking area and started taking out the delicious-smelling food from the bags. That was all she needed to forget her train of thought and answer her stomach that had suddenly leapt into service. Between bites of egg and cheese sandwiches and deep fried potatoes, Jerry and Willy filled her in on their interesting morning so far. They had checked out the local archives via Willy's computers and found some very interesting facts about the Kanes. They, of course, were from Ireland, as her ancestors were. But they also had family connections way back to Washford, as Jerry had said earlier. They in turn had their own Irish connections, which dated back to the ancient Celts and prior to that, the Dead Sea and beyond.

"Dead sea? You mean as in…the Dead Sea? As in Copper Scrolls, Qumran and all that stuff?" she interrupted her words barely audible over a big bite of English muffin.

"Uh huh. And what's more, the scrolls were really the beginning of the end of the Catholic Church's control over certain documentation. The truth was beginning to leak out. Dangerous truths," said Willy, equally animated. "You are connected to these truths!"

"Me? How is that?" she asked as she looked from one man to the other, taking a sip of her coffee.

"Well," said Jerry, picking up the story. "First I need to ask you something." He set his coffee down and looked at her intently. When she lifted her palms, hands in front of her, waiting for the answer, he asked, "Do you have a birthmark?"

She replied simply, "Yes."

"Where is it?"

"On my left shoulder, about two inches above my heart. Why?"

Can I see it?" Willy asked. When they both turned to look at him, he chuckled. "What can I say? A chance to see the bare shoulder of a beautiful young lady is a big thing to an old man!"

Without taking her eyes off Willy, she sighed heavily and pulled aside her t-shirt to reveal a star-shaped birthmark. "How the hell did I miss that?" said Jerry as he reached forward across the table to touch it and examine it further. Eliza smacked his hand away just as he was about to do a personal examination that she wasn't comfortable with in front of Willy.

"Down, boy!" She eyed him crossly and then smiled. "Is it that you were, shall we say, otherwise occupied at the time?"

Looking into his eyes, they both remembered the last time they were naked together a couple of days ago. She believed his thoughts took the same direction, as they smoldered and her breath caught. When Willy cleared his throat, she pulled the t-shirt back into place and they both came back to the present. Jerry sat down.
Eliza cleared her throat and stood up and left the table to pace the kitchen area.

"Listen, I don't mean to be rude or anything, Willy, but what does this birthmark have to do with all of this? This is an unbelievable scenario we've been innocently caught up in these past couple of days. What about the murders, the killings, the madmen chasing us?" She balled her hands into fists and wanted to punch something really bad. Shaking suddenly with suppressed fear and rage, she was pleading with them to give her answers. She needed them. Expected them. Wanted them. No! She wanted all of this to disappear! She wanted her life back. She wanted Dorothy to still be alive. She wanted those 43 people to still be alive. It was suddenly too much for her to comprehend and she crumpled to the floor, crying hysterically.

"Take her upstairs creep, while I make an herbal tea to relax her." Willy got up and went to the cooking area. He took out a kettle and some herbs to make the tea while Jerry knelt down and swung Eliza's sobbing body up into his arms and headed up the stairs to their room.

## Chapter 16

X-ray and Delta met with Agent Zero at the Royal York in downtown Toronto in the top penthouse suite at exactly two o'clock. The door was answered on the first knock, and they were shown into a paneled room with the shades drawn by an unknown government agent.

Agent Zero sat at a desk and looked up from his paperwork as the men entered. He set down his pen and folded his hands in front of him on the papers. "Gentlemen, please have a seat. You may leave us now," he said to the other man who quietly left the room to an adjoining suite and shut the door behind him.

Once the door was closed Zero turned his attention back to the two agents in front of him. "First things first," he said, addressing them in a controlled voice.

"Just so you know, we haven't lost their trail. I am in touch with their protector at the moment. The man who was found in the woman's apartment was none other than Mabus, the infamous terrorist from God knows where exactly! If nothing else, we are glad to be rid of him. He has murdered thousands of people for his governments and his own gain. He does this for no other reason than to make the world believe his government's belief system is the only one. So strongly do they believe this that they are trying to take over the world by any means possible. Of course, we all know someone else will be jumping up to take his place, but hopefully it will be a while before he or she starts their own terror campaign, and will give us sufficient time to find out who they are and take him out before these two are killed."

"But I thought that was what we were supposed to do!" interrupted Delta.

Holding his hand up to silence the agent, Zero reached inside a folder underneath his pile of paperwork and drew out a picture of Mabus and handed the picture and the government dossier to the agents seated.

"Okay, time for a brief history lesson. It is time you two were brought up to snuff as our people are now being taken out. The CIA, as you either may or may not know, hired Mabus back in the '70s. What you don't know is that he was hired to help protect the Davidic line. What the CIA didn't know was that Mabus was a triple agent and worked for anyone who met his price. So while pretending to be a protector, he was actually what some call the saviour of some Islamic extremists. He was a double agent for the CIA and a triple agent for the Cooperative at the same time! Busy guy, hmmm? He has helped orchestrate terrorist bombings, genocides and so on around the world since 1978. That is, until today, when he finally met his maker. It is the Cooperative's belief that the Davidic line must be eliminated. It poses too great a threat to their belief system. JPK's Irish families were from the Davidic line, as was Washford's, and so on back down through history. These men were assassinated by this terrorist group, who you may not know was hired by the first Pope…none other than the Apostle Peter, who took over after the crucifixion of Christ. It is our belief and many others that Peter was not to be the head of the Church. But Jesus' wife, Mary, was to lead his followers instead. Before you say anything, though," he held up his hand to the men, knowing they had millions of questions, "let me continue."

They nodded their ascent, and Zero toyed with his gold pen before resuming the story. "All right then," he said and set the pen down again on top of his paperwork. "Moving forward a bit, another leader of the free world, as we call it, was going to bring an end to its own countries Civil War by telling the masses his link to Jesus, believing it would bring a peace not known to man since the time of Adam. This couldn't happen as far as the Cooperative order was concerned, so he, too, was killed. They were confident the issue was now dead. Then they discover this leader had more family. He had links to a strong Catholic Irish family, the Kanes! This leader left a journal to his wife to be read upon his death. When she did finally read it a few years later, she contacted the family in Ireland who then immigrated to Canada. They were given a lot of land and money by the government to educate themselves and train to be politicians and leaders of the free world. Unfortunately the extremists also found this information out through their agents, and since that time almost every family member of the Kane family has met with early deaths. There is only one surviving member now, and she has no children, so their link is now a dead end.

"We are followers of the teachings of Paul, Thomas and James, who was the brother of Jesus, and tried to stop Peter and his cronies from spreading the lies, but were unsuccessful. Our job is and always has been to protect them, the last surviving members of the Davidic lineage, until the true saviour comes to power. Our estimated guess is, according to my source, that this is about 20 years from now. A great happening of this magnitude hasn't happened since the death of Jesus 2,000 years ago. The truth about Jesus and his lineage has been leaking out little by little since the Dead Sea Scrolls were discovered in 1947, and the Church had to do some backtracking. Ever read any Greek or Celtic mythology?"

Seeing the men look at each other with puzzled expressions, he went on.

"Uh, never mind. Let's go on then, shall we?" Clearing his throat and taking a sip of water, he said to them, "More and more people are questioning the Bible these days, which was written in code to protect the Davidic line long ago. Peter had the New Testament re-written to conform to his views and discredit James and Paul, erasing any mention of Jesus being married to Mary Magdalene and having children. He thereby eliminated the Davidic line. These lies also kept men in power in the Church in Rome, and at the same time reduced the role of women in the Church to mere bystanders. As I said earlier, we believe that Mary was to lead the Church, that she is of the Goddess line and is the real link and the mother of us all. The Goddess is equal in her power to the male God, but this contravenes all that we have ever been force-fed to believe. Therefore, the information has been squashed since the first century in all but the pagan circles." Taking a shaky breath and looking into the two stunned faces of his men, he wondered how much more they could ingest, but he had to tell them everything.

"But getting back to the Apostle James…there was nothing James could do about the lies, as Peter had him branded a heretic and then had him murdered. So, therefore, the true information of Christ and his ancestors remained hidden until Qumran was discovered. When Qumran was discovered, an archaeologist by the name of Pierre Robichaud was given charge by the Church to take over the dig and report his findings. They must have found something, as when the man went in for a minor surgery a few years into the dig, spies infiltrated the hospital and they made sure he never woke up, therefore silencing forever what he may have found as evidence to support the Davidic claim in today's century. "Following me so far?" he asked the men, who were trying to take it all in.

They shook their heads in unison. They had never heard this detailed account before! Oh, sure, there were rumours and television programs, but they were all suppositions, right? Who were they anyway? They were simply soldiers doing good deeds on behalf of the government of the USA, or so they thought, not embroiled in some good versus evil thing. They nodded in unison, even though the plot was getting foggier by the moment.

"OK," said Zero, rubbing the crease between his brows. God, he had a headache, but hoped it would ease soon enough once the pain medication kicked in. These two men were close. Close, he felt, to touching something men had dreamed about for 2,000 years: the fact that the couple they were shadowing were actual descendants of the Davidic line and between them would produce the new messiah! Sighing deeply, Zero continued with the amazing story.

"Prime Minister Kane knew he was a descendant of this sacred line, but somehow he also knew that the Messiah for the new Millennium would not come directly from him or his cursed family, so he felt he was safe telling his secrets to Olga Hanson. What he didn't know was that she had another lover: Charity Stringer. Olga told everything to Charity, who chronicled it all into three journals. Olga had also kept a diary, which we found and destroyed. It didn't really have that much in it. Certainly not enough to warrant killing her, but I didn't make the decisions back then. We were unable to find Charity's journals. The cleaners who set up her "suicide" botched the job and had to leave her house when the husband came home early. He found her dead, sitting up in bed, and after her funeral, after going through her things, we believe he found these journals and hid them away. They had one child, named Dorothy. Dorothy never married, and her father died "by accidental means," if you get my drift. He was trying to sell the journals when we got wind of it. We are sure she found these journals hidden among his things after he died. We believe she traced the link to Eliza McPhelimy, who has deep Celtic roots. Dorothy took a job at the Toronto City Tribune not long after Eliza was hired, and they became good friends. From what we have been able to ascertain, Dorothy had not told Eliza about the link. She had no clue. If she had we would have overheard it. She probably knows by now that she is, in fact, a direct descendant of this Davidic line, as is this Jerry Malloy. We have to get to them before the group hires more replacement killers. So this leads me now to you two! Tell me what you have learned." He sat back in his leather chair and waited to hear the report from what was now his only hope of saving the Davidic line. For what they didn't know was if these two were killed, the lineage would end right here and now and the world would be doomed.

# Chapter 17

Jerry laid Eliza on the soft coverlet and tried his best to console her. Willy came in shortly after carrying a tray with three mugs of steaming tea on it. "This one is for her," said Willy quietly as he handed the mug to Jerry. "It will calm her. Once she is resting, you and I need to talk."

About a half hour later Jerry came downstairs and located Willy at the far end of the living room, clicking away on a computer keyboard, lost in thought. This guy is always surprising me, thought Jerry. What isn't he in to these days? "Computer whiz" would have been far down on the list!

He went over to stand beside Willy, who gestured he pull up another office chair and continued typing without interruption. When he finally paused he looked sideways at his friend and grinned. "What is it? You've got that…"I know something you don't know" look, old man!"

"Yep, and it's true, creep! I guess I need to fill you in on a few things. You think me an old man. Maybe a stupid native, perhaps?" Shaking his head he said, "Never stupid, Willy, never that!"

Willy paused and smiled at the young man with appreciation and continued. "OK, we agree on the 'old' part then?" When Jerry nodded his agreement and drank some more tea, Willy smiled at his friend and continued.

"You and I have known each other not long in human years, but we have known each other hundreds of years through past lives." He held up his hand when he felt Jerry was going to interrupt him again. "Please let me finish. This is going to take a bit of discussing." When Jerry nodded silently, he spoke again.

"First of all, let me tell you my real name. It's not Willy. I mean, what native guy would have a name like that? But you whiteys need easy to pronounce ones so…"

"So? What is your name then?" asked Jerry, looking annoyed at another new discovery.

"My real name is Gete Zhmaagan, which in my native language means 'old warrior.' So now can you now see why I use the name Willy?

"Yeah, I can. Wow! Gete, eh? Interesting name and it suits you." Slapping the old guy on the back, he encouraged him to continue with his story.

"OK, now to more important stuff! You probably don't recognize these characters here I am typing on the screen, do you?" He gestured to the computer screen. When Jerry answered no, he said, "They look like Egyptian hieroglyphs, but they are not. They are actually an ancient text very few can decipher today, but I am one of them. I use this form of writing, as it's a great code that cannot be broken. I actually used it in the Second World War to help the allies win against the Germans! Don't look so surprised, my friend! There is more to me than meets the eye," he said as a smile touched his lips. He added more text to the screen.

"I actually learned it in the early fourteenth century!" Gete stopped typing to gauge the young man's response, and he wasn't disappointed.

Jerry turned white as a sheet and said, "No shit? This day keeps getting better and better. What other surprises do you have for me?"

Gete turned back to the computer screen and started to type again. "What you see here is a conversation between me and a man we all call Zero. Strange name for a white man! It means 'nothing,' but then again, that is what he wants to be, 'nothing,' not traceable, not recordable. He has had a couple of his agents trailing you and Eliza since the death of that reporter."

"You mean they aren't the ones trying to kill us?"

"Well, not now, no." Seeing the confusion bubble out of Jerry's sputtering mouth, he put a reassuring hand on his shoulder and squeezed. "You have to know they had bogus info on you, which they don't have now thanks to my contacting them. You see, there is something I know that even you don't! You, too, have this famous birthmark. It's on the right side of your chest just below the breastbone. I saw it earlier when we went for a swim in the pool. Didn't you know you had this?"

Jerry didn't know what to think. What the hell? He had a Davidic birthmark? Him? His family was French so this didn't make sense!

"Yeah," he agreed, nodding his head. "I have seen it before! But it is only a blob, not a star like Eliza's. I think whoever they are have made a mistake here, Willy."

"Mind you," old Willy said with a chuckle, "yours isn't as pretty as hers is!"

He then added, "You are now probably thinking this is wrong, as you are French, and the Davidic line dates back to the Celts, right? Well, where do you think the history of the Celts came from? France! I met many displaced Celts in France. Anyway, in addition, your surname is Malloy, and I can confirm it used to be O'Mall in Ireland. Just as I can confirm McPhelimy used to be Mcphellmea. There were a few different spellings over the years, but trust me, you both are the descendants of these two Celtic families."

Jerry sat in stunned silence, unable to respond. Do brains actually explode? he wondered. His brain felt like it was about to!
"You and Eliza are the only surviving children of the House of David Actually, it pre-dates David's lineage, but to make it easier to comprehend we started the writings there, except for one document that shows it all the way back." Willy continued as he saw the dawn of realization flowing across Jerry's features.

"If you must know, we call it the 'Davidic Lineage,' but it is actual Pagan, as paganism was the first known form of worship of the God and Goddess. Dorothy found out about the connection to Eliza, but not about you. You just happened, not by accident I might add, to be the one to find her. The guys who killed her were protecting the line. They thought she was going to exploit it in the newspapers, but all she wanted to do was tell Eliza, and she never got the chance. We have no idea why she didn't tell her, but perhaps she knew we were onto her and she wanted to protect her. What Zero now tells me is that guy who showed up at your girlfriend's place was part of several terrorist cell networks that has been around since the first century. They have been the ones who have been murdering any links to this line to protect their version of what religion is. They don't want the truth to get out. You both were not supposed to survive. The fact that you have survived is more than a miracle. You two are the miracle!"

"What do we do now, Willy? Or should I call you Gete now that I know Willy isn't your real name?" He was suddenly so angry he could spit. The world was nuts, crazy, upside down, and he was in the centre of it all!

"Willy will be just fine," Gete quietly responded.

"Willy, are you now saying these fucking lunatics believe we, Eliza and me, are the new Mary and Joseph reborn? This is fucking nuts!"

Jerry didn't usually swear, so the fact he was doing so now surprised, revolted and exhilarated him at the same time. Just saying the words released some of the pent-up emotions he was swilling in. He paced the floor back and forth as he pounded one fisted hand into the other. He looked like a fighter about to enter the ring. But whom was he fighting against? Willy? A shadow government? Or a mysterious Agent Zero? Who calls themselves that in this day and age anyway??

"I am who I say I am. And when Eliza awakes I will tell you more," came Willy's somber reply. He remained seated during the young man's tirade. He deserved to shout, to curse, to swear! Who wouldn't in his shoes? From this point onward both of their lives, the lives they thought they would control, would never be the same. He typed a coded message to Zero and gave him directions to his place. The most important thing to do now was to get these kids to a safe country where their child, the one they didn't know had been conceived, could be born and protected until it was able to reveal itself to the world.

## Chapter 18

Eliza awoke some time later to a darkened bedroom. She had no idea how long she had slept, but she felt refreshed for the first time in days. She heard the strains of classical music waft up from the rooms down below. She loved baroque music and recognized a melody of Bach's Fifth Symphony right away. She almost allowed it to lull her back to sleep. Sighing, she threw back the comforter and slid off the bed. Her feet melted at once into the wonderful carpeting. Picking up a robe, which someone had thoughtfully laid on the chair beside the bed, she went in search of her bag. God, she felt good! What the hell was in the tea anyway?

After finding her bag at the foot of the bed, she rummaged through it until she picked out clean underwear, khaki shorts and a white blouse, and headed toward the bathroom. Like most things in Willy's house, it, too, had an abundance of pine throughout. The long vanity had a green marble top with brass fixtures. The two-person shower was encased in a tempered glass shell, with native motifs etched into the glass. It was breathtakingly beautiful. So much so that she spent a few minutes running her fingers over the precious carvings, letting her thoughts wander to the beasts portrayed there. There was a prowling bear with a freshly caught fish in its claws; a perched owl, it's all-seeing eyes taking in the world around him; the female doe, frolicking in the mist; and a beaver gnawing down trees. Each had it's own special significance to the Native people. The warrior depicted on one side of the stall was a mystery, though. Shrugging any explanation off, and without another thought of the etchings, she stepped inside the huge basin and turned on the water. She had already stripped out of her clothes, and she let her body melt under the soft, tepid water. She washed away the grief, the anger and the silt that seemed to permeate her very being. The amenities that Willy provided were very luxurious. The shampoo and conditioner were top of the line, as was the eucalyptus shower gel. She could have stayed in there indefinitely, but knew at some point she had to step back into this new reality that was her life now. She had questions that needed answers, and by God Willy was going to give them to her one way or the other. She toweled off and walked back into the bedroom, nude, to get dressed. She left the fluffy robe where she dropped it beside the shower doors.

A full moon shone in through the patio windows and she thought this was as good a time as any to draw a bit of the Mother into herself. It had been a long time since she had done a Moon ritual, and her body now intensely craved it. She strode out onto the private deck and raised her face and arms to the full moon. She basked in its glow and reveled in the energies that her body soaked in. The words spoken long ago fell from her lips as she spoke in the ancient Celtic tongue few would recognize.

She finished with "so mote it be," and lowered her arms to her sides. She felt full inside, bursting with life and love. She was complete. This connection to the Goddess was something no man would ever completely understand. Oh, yes, there were male witches, but they could never connect to the Mother as a daughter would, as far as she was concerned. As she stood there, naked and open to the universe, she decided while she was at it to ask for help and called upon the Goddess Hecate. If anyone was plotting to do her harm, this would end it, she hoped, or at least right those who have been wronged! This was a chance she hadn't been given previously, except for a brief attempt at contacting Jerry telepathically at the apartment.

She lifted her arms again and once more spoke the memorized words to the universe as below her, evil stalked silently.

> Goddess Hecate, Goddess of mine
> I stand before thee in the silver moon's shine—
> sleeping beneath the black velvet seas
> I summon thee
> I allow the anger to run through my veins—
> knowing it will be you who keeps me sane—
> you will come to my aid in a blaze of light
> wielding your sword of great powers with might
> they will fall to their knees in fright!
> As you rise from the underworld this night
> wise one, my protector, old crone
> knowing you are here I am never alone…
> I can face all the evil that is thrown at me
> as our mirror images meld as one by the power of three
> I call upon you to enter now
> rest your weary heart upon my brow strike at those who
> do me harm let their blood flow red and warm!
> Come now, my goddess, come to me.
> On feathered wings, blessed be
> I cry out to you in need
> only you can set me free

The wind came up swiftly and abruptly, whipping her hair about her face as she spoke the words softly to the cosmos. Her arms were still raised and her body was still warm from the brief ritual, so she did not feel the chill as it surrounded the house.

Willy did, though, and quickly jumped up and away from the computer desk. So hastily, in fact, did he move, that Jerry thought perhaps some invisible force had propelled him backward! When Willy stood, his chair toppled backward onto the carpet with a thud.

"What is it, old man? Some big bug going to bite you or something?" he asked, chuckling.

"A force is here," Willy replied, quietly looking around him. Jerry knew from one glance that the old man wasn't seeing things with the same eyes as he was.

"Something or someone has come that is not welcome." His weathered voice took on a slight sound of fear for the very first time. Jerry felt as if something evil was going to materialize out of thin air.

Jerry followed Willy's lead, roaming around the huge room. He didn't feel, see or sense anything that would indicate any supernatural, physical or ghostly prescience. But he was not skilled in that area of course, and had to trust the old man's instincts, which he knew where never wrong.

Instead, he intently watched his old friend as he continued to see or hear something his human senses could not. The old warrior continued to circle the living room and then stood stock-still and raised his arms, chanting words in Ojibway that would have been unfamiliar to Jerry if Willy hadn't repeated the English words right after the Ojibway ones.

Gzhemnido, gchi-miigwech kina gegoo gii miizhiyang. gchi-miigwech gii miizhiyang iw sa bimaadziwin, wiidookwishnaag noomgom, gaawin zegzisii miinwaa wiidookwishnaang gwayak ji bimooseyaang. kina ndinwendaaganag

Great Spirit, thank you for all that you give us. Thank you for this life you have given. Help us today not to be afraid and help us to walk a straight path, all my relations.

After the words were spoken, a loud crash came from outside the house and the old man broke free from his trance. Jerry joined him as they ran out of the house to see what had caused the noise. What they found astounded even them. A few feet beyond the driveway, a huge maple tree had fallen. Underneath the tree, barely visible, was what once was a vehicle. Even thought it was hard to see in the dark of night, there was still enough light from the full moon for them to know it had been a car that didn't belong there. Together they quickly ran toward the automobile and peered through the broken tree limbs into the front seat of the crushed car. It was a telltale sedan, and the occupants were not covert, of that they could be sure. There were two men inside. Not Caucasian, as most government bodies were, but of Middle Eastern descent. Both bodies were obviously broken, from the way they were half sitting and half lying on the front seat. The tree had literally crushed the roof of the car down upon them. It must have happened swiftly, as they had no time to react or escape. They sat wide-eyed, with their guns still in their hands, as if they were about to get out and come after them. And in one split second, their lives were over. Willy grabbed his cell phone from the belt strap on his jeans and rapidly jammed in a series of numbers on the keypad. The call was answered immediately.

The discussion was intense, that much he could tell, even if the old guy was speaking quickly in his Ojibway language, He ended the call and, closing his cell phone, reattached it to his belt and turned back toward the house.

"Someone will be here shortly to take this away," he said, gesturing to the wreck. Without asking Jerry to join him, he walked back toward the house. Jerry looked back at the car and the dead men, with their blood-covered faces and their wide-eyed stares. He closed his own eyes, trying to block out the horrific scene. It was going to be difficult thing to do, if he was ever able to do it, and he followed his friend back inside the house.

Eliza, unaware of the commotion, was upstairs on the deck, reveling in the night breeze that floated across her body. She was totally immersed in the warmth that chanting to the Goddess always gave her. And then suddenly the wind died and she heard the crash somewhere outside. She couldn't see anything from her vantage point, so she stepped back inside and quickly dressed and ran downstairs. She met Willy at the front door.

"What happened? I heard a crash and then…" She was cut short when she saw Willy's face, which had gone as white as a native's skin could. "Is it…is Jer…is he…? Oh God!"

Then Jerry walked in the front door a few paces behind the old man. She ran into his arms and kissed his face over and over, thanking God he was OK. She had thought he was dead by the look on Willy's face.

He hugged her back and steered her toward one of the leather couches, slowly lowering her there so he could disentangle himself from her death grip.

"Easy, girl. We had some company we weren't expecting, and it appears that nature took care of them."

"What do you mean 'company'? Nature? I don't understand!" she shrieked, looking from one man to the other.

Willy calmly walked up to Eliza and put one finger under her chin. She lifted her face to his as he asked, "Did you call on the Goddess tonight, Eliza?" When she only nodded an affirmative, never taking his eyes off his, Willy walked over to a tall bookcase nestled in one corner of the room neither she nor Jerry had noticed before, and withdrew a huge old book.

Finding her voice after watching him extract the weird-looking book, she said, "Uh, well…yeah…okay, I did." She was a bit embarrassed that he would know about something she considered to be so personal.

"Why?" she asked, looking from one man to the other.

## Chapter 19

Agent Zero took the urgent call from Willy immediately and, after hanging up the phone, addressed the two men in his hotel office.

"The Cooperative was able to get replacements quicker than we expected, it seems. A freak tree fell outside of Willy's house up North and has just crushed two guys of Middle Eastern descent. We can only surmise they were part of the same family that Mabus emerged from. KGB and MI5 have confirmed this. I think it's time we brought CSIS into the fold, as I'll need to explain to them why I am relocating two entire families to foreign countries without the proper paperwork! I need you two to leave immediately and provide outside protection. Are we all clear about your real God mission now?"

He looked from one man to the other who, after their long, enlightening discussion with their boss, now had a new duty in life. They were to be charged with protecting the life of a new messiah.

Who would have believed this to be possible? But it was true, and both knew this was only the beginning of new chapters of their own lives. Instead of being hired guns eliminating others to protect global security, they would now be guarding the future king of the world! They both verbally affirmed their understanding and stood to shake hands with Zero. They left the room, quieting shutting the door behind them. They had been given directions to Willy's and access to enough money and safe houses to last their lifetimes.

After exiting the hotel's underground parking lot a few minutes later, they took the quickest exit to the 401 westbound, which would hook them up to Highway 400, then up Highway 11 from Orillia to Washago. It would be a short drive to Willy's from there.

# Chapter 20

"What else did you do, Eliza, when you invoked the Goddess?" Willy asked as he watched her intently. His powerful grey eyes never left her face. Jerry looked from one to the other, not quite understanding why this information was so important, so he kept quiet so he wouldn't interrupt the link they seemed to have at the moment.

"I also invoked the Goddess Hecate," she answered softly. "I thought since we had been in so much danger that her protection would be an added bonus." She felt nervous now under his scrutiny and started to fidget with her pentagram necklace.

"Aha...now this makes sense. Your Hecate Goddess, she works fast, little one. We have much to fill you in on."

And so Willy told a startled Eliza about her direct link to the past; how Jerry was also linked; about meeting their ancestors; about the lost journals, which meant nothing now; and how they would have to leave here soon and spend the rest of their lives in safe-houses. "Why us? I mean...why now? Why I am finding this out now? Why didn't my parents tell me this or Jer's parents tell him."

It was a logical question, and she hoped it was going to be a logical answer. Jerry nodded and looked to Willy and asked him, "Yeah, Willy! Why didn't our parents tell us this?"

"They most likely didn't know! Their parents didn't tell them and so on. I would guess Eliza that your great-great-

great-grand-mother knew the truth. She was an awesome lass, if I may say so! She and I were, ahem, quite close! She was pretty much the only person I ever confided in, as I knew it was going to take until the twenty-first century for these events to take place. By telling too many, it would have placed too many people in danger. Only those in the "need to know" business such as MI5, CIA, FBI and KGB have known about all of this pretty much since the beginning. Of course, back then, there was no MI5, but there were organizations such as the Masons Templar's and so forth."

"I knew it was going to be you, Eliza. Where there is female there is male, so when I saw Jerry's birthmark, it all fit. They, the governments, knew enough about you, if not by name, from Olga Hanson's journals. They were tapping Dorothy's phone and computers files, so they knew that she had her mom's journals and also that she knew the truth about you or one of your family members. When Dorothy took the job at the newspaper, it all fell into place. They felt she was going to divulge the news to you, and so her days were numbered. Why they didn't want you to know is beyond me. It has been my mission in life to protect this book until I can pass it along to its rightful owners. As far as your families…you will not be able to see them again unless it is through secure channels. They are also being taken to safe houses and protected for the remainder of their lives. When he saw the anger surface on their faces when talk of their families enduring danger was mentioned, he said. "Think! How better to get to you if they kidnap your families! You are their only children. Would they not do anything in their power to protect you?" When he saw realization dawn on their faces, he spoke on.

"They have been picked up already by associates of Agent Zero, and your parents," he motioned to Eliza, "are on their way to Switzerland. Yours," he turned to Jerry, "are on their way to a lovely country estate in southern France. Trust me, they will be well cared for. You both will see them as often as is possible."

He paused for effect when they tore their eyes away from each other and looked at the old man. "And you are with child, Eliza."

"Oh, now you've gone too far." Eliza jumped up from the couch and rounded on the men. "How the hell could this be possible? And how do you know this? How the hell do you know this?"

She asked Willy again, "What are you, some type of psychic or something? No!" She held up her hand as he opened his mouth to speak. "Let me guess! You are an old spiritualist, right? You are given visions from your Great Spirit, and you have great powers to control the universe…am I getting warm? Oh, yeah, and I forgot you had a fling with an ancestor of mine whose been dead two hundred years!"

She was livid. How dare this old coot deceive her after all they had been through? He didn't seem the type. She stopped ranting long enough to think. But what if she was pregnant? She would know if she was pregnant, wouldn't she? What if she was, though, she thought as her hand strayed to her still flat stomach. What if she was?

The rest of the night passed in a haze for her. The two men Willy told her were coming arrived around three a.m. and took up their lookout spots outside the house. Jerry drove her, with the agents following close behind, to the pharmacy the next day in Washago. They bought a home pregnancy test. It confirmed what the old Indian had told her the night before. She was indeed pregnant. Just pregnant, mind you, but pregnant for sure! A range of emotions tore through her: Happiness, sadness, elation, horror. Finally, after a few hours, she accepted the deck of cards that they had all been dealt.

Willy, they discovered, had somehow met the ancient Knights Templar's. This was the reason for all of his knowledge and when he handed them an ancient text it all fit together. What he gave them was the very first book of truth. The very first book of our genealogy. What it was called then was the "Book of Ages." It was beautiful. It must have been six inches thick or more, with a wood cover embellished with Celtic glyphs written on the front in gold. Each page was written on vellum and the text was actual gold letters. The drawings were exquisite. Eliza sucked in a breath when she found a sketch of a woman from the second century who could have been her twin. Likewise, she saw a man who resembled Jerry. It was like nothing either of them had ever seen before in real life or in a movie. The true Holy Grail! The book proved without a doubt that there was a lineage with links back to the first Pagan rituals. It was her lineage. His lineage! The child she now carried would be born in eight months and would be the next messiah, the new saviour of their world.

He would be born on December 21, the celebration of the Pagan festival of Yule. This was the true date of Christmas and the date of the birth of the son, the messiah.

Jerry looked over at her as she rested in the back seat of the dark blue sedan, the same one they had been fleeing from, and watched her as she slept. There was a glow about her now that wasn't evident before, and he knew he would do anything and everything in his power to ensure she stayed safe. The child would stay safe until he would be old enough to reveal his true identity to the world. Willy watched as the car pulled out of the drive. He was happy in knowing that at last his charges were in safe hands. Now he could decide what he wanted to do with his own life. It hadn't really been his until now. He thought back several hundred years to when he was travelling through France at the time of the great massacre of the Knights Templar. He remembered how he came across the chateau; he remembered the raid during the night and how he was saved by three Templar's who dangled him off a cliff in order to save his life. The men, knowing their time was short, gave Willy the book, their Holy Grail, and told him to keep it safe. He had done this successfully! He had lived to see the day when the new leader of the free world would rise from the dust. They told him how they had indeed found the elixir of life. The Holy Grail wasn't a cup, but this book instead, one that gave humankind the truth they had long sought after and would one day be intelligent enough to digest once the contents were revealed. Now was not the time, though. There was too much unrest, too much evil in the world. They placed the book in Gete's hands and a warm glow filled his body. The Templar's told him that whoever held the book and kept it under their protection from evil did not die but lived until the Grail was placed into its rightful owner's hands.

So many years had passed. He didn't know how long he was going to wait to find the true owners of the book after the first four hundred years had passed. But a fleeting vision from one of the Templar's as he slept gave him the knowledge he sought, and he had waited for this moment to arrive for so long. But now he was suddenly very tired. Seven hundred years was a long time to wait for this turn of event, but then again, he had a hot tub, a pool and tons of money to keep him happy for the next 20 years or so. Perhaps the Goddess would bless him, knowing that he had completed his duty with love and devotion, and would allow him to live long enough to see the messiah rise to power and bring final peace to this earth. Much had been done and many lives had been lost and saved. With one final wave at the disappearing car, he turned back toward his home. A smile played upon his lips as he whispered before he, and everything around him faded into the mist, "Wait until they discover their messiah is female! All hell's gonna break loose!"

## The End

….or is it only the beginning?